FIRST EXECUTION

Domenico Starnone

FIRST EXECUTION

*Translated from the Italian
by Antony Shugaar*

Europa
editions

Europa Editions
116 East 16th Street
New York, N.Y. 10003
www.europaeditions.com
info@europaeditions.com

Copyright © by Giangiacomo Feltrinelli Editore, Milano
First Publication 2009 by Europa Editions

Translation by Antony Shugaar
Original title: *Prima esecuzione*
Translation copyright © 2009 by Europa Editions

Library of Congress Cataloging in Publication Data is available
ISBN 978-1-933372-66-2

Starnone, Domenico
First Execution

Book design by Emanuele Ragnisco
www.mekkanografici.com

Prepress by Plan.ed – Rome

Printed in the United States of America

For Lucia, and Matilde

FIRST EXECUTION

1.

When I heard that Nina had been arrested, I called her parents. Her mother answered the phone; she started crying. I tried to find the right words to comfort her; I told her that politically it was an ugly time; I railed against the habit of criminalizing anyone willing to stand up for the rights of the weak. I only hung up when I felt confident she had calmed down.

Time passed and I was told that the girl had returned home. I felt obliged to make another phone call; I spoke to a man who sounded young—perhaps her brother—and asked about Nina. He thanked me for my concern but said that she didn't want to speak to anyone. I felt a sense of relief. I had grown old doing not what I wanted to do, but rather what corresponded to the way I saw myself. I asked the young man to tell Nina her old literature professor was by her side.

A couple of weeks later, Nina's father called me and the minute I heard his voice I thought back to the time that he had scolded me, with shy determination, for the influence I exerted upon his daughter.

This time the phone call was terse, unceremonious, just the facts: Nina was fine, she was living in her apartment in Talenti again, she'd like to see me. I said that I'd be glad to see her as well, and arranged a meeting for the following morning, at ten.

I was up early. At seven thirty on the dot I had already breakfasted and read the newspaper, and I was washing up in the kitchen, listening to the radio. I thought about Nina. Once, during class, it struck me that not only was she paying no attention, she was making a point of it, as if she were acting out her decision to ignore me in a stage play. So I said something to her, a gentle reprimand. She rolled her eyes sarcastically and replied with the faintest woof of indifference, barely audible a foot away: "So?" I rebuked her in a cold and threatening tone, but she still showed no fear. On the contrary, the whole time I spoke to her, she stared straight at me, unwavering, and continued to hiss at me: "So? so? so?" emotionlessly drowning out every word I said. She stopped only when I gave in. The expression on her face belonged to someone who would never surrender, whom you would have to kill.

I couldn't reconstruct the subject of that day's lesson. There have been times, during my career as a teacher, and increasingly often in the last decade before retiring, when I suspected that I was saying things I'd never been thoroughly convinced of. Perhaps Nina had sensed it, and she'd thrown it in my face in that pitiless way of hers. Anyway, from that moment on she was my favorite student.

I switched off the radio and sat down at the kitchen table in the silent apartment. Perhaps I'd been too indulgent with her, and with all the other students like her. My wife had often told me, until just before the day she died, that she found me most exasperating when I was being indulgent, indulgent with a hint of arrogance. Our daughters felt the same way; it raised their hackles that I always reacted to their most reckless actions with a patient tone of affection. Even I felt a vague sense of annoyance at the words dripping with kindly omniscience that I regularly spoke to my students, my family, to everyone. It felt as if the answers I kept in constant readiness, answers that, now I was getting old, I continued to repeat, word for word, were meant especially to ward off questions that might bewilder me.

I left for the meeting in a bad mood.

2.

I had a hard time recognizing her. Around the girl I remembered—a slender adolescent, mouth always half-open, a serious, profound gaze, a way of dressing that was never fashionable but nonetheless refined—there had accumulated layers of an older woman, puffy-faced, no makeup, wearing jeans and a sweater that seemed too light for the chilly March weather. She stood in front of the newsstand under a light drizzle, smoking nervously.

We shook hands, kissed cheeks, and hastened into a café. I cast a glance at the pastries; I had developed a sweet tooth in the past few years. Nina followed my gaze and grimaced with revulsion.

When we had seated ourselves at a little table squeezed in between merciless mirrors, she glanced briefly at her own reflection but soon wrenched her eyes away, saying that she wanted only an espresso.

She must have sensed that in order to recognize her I'd been obliged to carve the Nina of ten years ago out of the material of her current appearance. And so, even as I was ordering a couple of beignets, she made an idle remark about the weight of a decade, whether the years crawl by or hurtle past.

"I'm twenty-eight, and I look like I'm forty," she remarked bitterly.

I shook my head to reassure her that she was overstating matters. She was no older than her years. I told her I was sixty-seven, an age at which you understand that the problem isn't how old you look but how old you are. "Science will reduce the weight of time," she quipped. I replied, feigning resignation, that it was too late for that. "The weight of the years has already broken my back."

We went on like that for a little while, trading barbs on my genuine old age, her apparent old age, the miracles of genetics, the importance of seeing to it—as society was already doing—that billions of human beings in the Third World, to the south, should be exterminated in order to allow others in the First World, to the north, to live longer and longer, and that their age should weigh ever more lightly upon them. I was hesitant to ask about her arrest, about the trouble she was in, and she certainly showed no interest in talking about it. So I sipped my tea, ate my two pastries, and chattered on, lingering on the chosen topic.

She didn't sugar her espresso; she tossed it back black and bitter in great gulps, looking away as I greedily ate my beignets. It was not until I mentioned the African hecatomb, those legions dying of AIDS, that she grimaced in annoyance and said: the same old routine, the things you said in class are the things you're saying now. I felt a wave of embarrassment, afraid that I was offering the sorry spectacle of an old man repeating himself, over and over. I wondered if my lips were smeared with frosting and I wiped my mouth with a paper napkin. Nina went on with a mocking smile: you always knew the number of victims of hunger, thirst, wars, Mafia, diseases, and multinationals. I muttered: "To know things was my job." "Hell of a job," she replied. "When you walked into the classroom, it was always as if a black cloud lowered over the desks."

I tried to make out if she was joking. No, she meant what she said. Her expression was ironic, there was amusement in her tone of voice, but underlying the things she said was clearly a memory of pain.

I asked her brusquely: "Don't you want to tell me about what happened? It's all settled, I hope."

She made a face, and then looked me straight in the eye.

"They don't have a thing against me."

"Well, I'm glad to hear it. I never doubted you were innocent."

"Why?"

"Because I know you. And because they let you go."

"I'm still under investigation."

"What for?"

"Armed conspiracy."

I said nothing. I knew nothing about the penal code, police investigations, criminal charges, or judicial procedure. Nina had been arrested along with a great many others. Before phoning her parents' house, I had spent a long while trying to imagine my eighteen-year-old student involved in acts that might have led in one way or another to the murder of innocent victims—acts ranging from trailing someone to aiming a gun and pulling the trigger. Nina—I had decided, with an upwelling sense of queasiness—would have been fully capable of any of those acts, moment after moment. All the same, as in so many other situations in my life, I could not bring myself to act is if I had never known her, as if I wasn't still fond of her.

"What can I do for you?"

"Are you sure that you want to do something for me?"

"Certainly."

"Why?"

"Because I am responsible for having educated you."

"Do you consider me a professional liability?"

"No."

"So? You did your job, and now you're done."

"To educate is a powerful, positive action, it establishes a bond that cannot be dissolved."

Nina smiled.

"You are so predictable."

"My daughters tell me the same thing."

"I'm not one of your daughters. I'm about to ask you something they'd never ask you to do."

"What?"

Her tone of voice grew serious.

"I need you to do what being arrested kept me from doing."

3

She asked me to go to the apartment of a friend of hers. The apartment had been empty for some time, her friend was overseas, she handed me the keys. On the bookshelves in the living room I would find a copy of *The Death of Virgil*, by Hermann Broch. On page 46 a few words had been underlined. I was to transcribe those words and place the sheet of paper in an envelope. Soon, someone would show up and ask for the envelope. That was all.

I said: "You know that the police are probably watching us." She smiled.

"No one's watching us. But let's say they are, where's the problem?"

"The problem is that I'll go to your friend's apartment, I'll copy the message onto a sheet of paper, and they'll arrest me right away."

"So?"

"They'll question me."

"And?"

"I don't understand you."

"There's nothing to understand. If you can't do this favor for me, just say so, I'll ask someone else."

I meant to tell her no, but I found myself saying yes. I did it to live up to her expectations.

"I'll let you know how it turns out," I said when we stepped back out into the street, into the rain. She shook her head, there was no need. It was clear that she never wanted to hear from me or see me again. She kissed me on both cheeks without affection and left.

As soon as she turned the corner, I put on my hat to keep from getting any wetter than I already was. As I walked along the street, on my way to pick up the results of the exams that Ida, my eldest daughter, had insisted I take, I asked myself one silent question after another. I wondered if she was trying to get me into trouble with the law because of some resentment dating from when she was a student. Or was she trying to reverse our roles and teach me something, something that eluded me now but would later become clear? And last of all, I asked myself whether perhaps I wasn't exaggerating a little: maybe all she wanted was one harmless favor, with no ulterior motives.

I thought it over for a long time, walking unhurriedly through the rain. I finally concluded that if she had been asking me to do something illegal, Nina—certainly not out of any concern for my well-being, but in order to ensure that the mission was successful—would never have sent me to a stranger's apartment, without precautions, recklessly. For that matter, hadn't she smiled that mocking smile of hers when I betrayed my sense of alarm? And hadn't she made it clear that I needn't worry; that is, about breaking the law?

I picked up the results of the tests, I checked my numbers, they all looked reassuring. That gave me a sense of well-being, I no longer felt an old pain in my knee, the swelling that I'd had in my right hip had vanished. When I stepped back out into the street, the rain had stopped.

I waited for the bus standing next to a sycamore; the tree roots had tunneled under the sidewalk, corrugating the asphalt. I imagined the living earth beneath the city's cement, a network of dark filaments linking one tree to another, coiling over underground artifacts from ancient eras, mosaics, paintings, statues, bones, and skulls, and then returning to the daylight, verdant, flowering in gardens, parks, and then sinking back down to concealment in the black depths. And in the meanwhile I felt a sudden urge to plunge my hands into the little patch of damp soil out of which the plane tree grew, to dig a tunnel down into the earth.

These were fantasies I had had as a boy. I dreamed of opening a breach in the darkness, liberating lives that slumbered, awaiting redemption. I read extensively, and not just novels. I was fascinated by books that spoke of injustice, I've been fascinated with them all my life. I have boxes filled with old files filled with information, files that I used to remind myself and others that the rich lives enjoyed by some were the fruit of the truncated, mutilated lives of the many.

I had begun to record information before I was twenty. I knew everything about living conditions in Latin America, Africa, and Asia. I had learned the names of everyone who had fought or was still fighting to improve those conditions. I studied world history to nourish my growing sense of indignation. I would torture myself with books about Nazi concentration camps, I had understood early that a country that creates prison camps, whatever it might say about itself, is a country heading in the wrong direction. I was on the side of the hungry, the thirsty, the poorly armed. I was on the side of all those afflicted with poverty, those who had died and were dying—horrifying statistics—as a result of our ferocious opulence. I loved the faces of the insurgents, hollowed out by hardships, the delirium in the large haunted eyes. My chest swelled with fury when I thought about the living conditions of most of humanity, and I said to myself—as I had said for decades to my students—that there are times when a person with any sensibility must sell his cloak and purchase a sword. All of a sudden, I was sorry that the task with which Nina had entrusted was not more compromising.

When I got back home, I looked first of all in my bookshelves to see if I had a copy of *The Death of Virgil*, though I was pretty certain I had never read it and therefore, most likely, never owned it. But I was always doing the same thing in recent years where book were concerned: I would check the shelves as if the book that I already knew wasn't there might suddenly appear as if by magic, or as if a book that I could swear had always been there might have suddenly mysteriously disappeared (stolen by a student who had dropped by, or borrowed without permission by my daughters).

After that, I phoned Ida and told her that my test results showed that I was in excellent shape. She demanded that I carefully read out the individual results to her over the phone, though she was a librarian, not a physician.

"What were you doing this morning?" she admonished me, with the usual tone in her voice of a disgruntled governess, while her youngest daughter shrilled in the background that she wanted to talk to me, "I called you and you weren't in, you had even turned off your cell phone."

"I went to pick up my test results."

"It took you that long to pick up your results?"

"I went for a walk."

"In the rain?"

"I had a hat and my umbrella."

"Papa, I'm warning you: if you get sick I'm not lifting a finger, I already have plenty of problems and I can't start taking care of you, too."

"I'm fine, I'm not Methuselah, you know."

That evening I decided to stop worrying and go over to the apartment of Nina's friend, who lived on Via Pavia. I examined the bunch of keys; there were five of them. Two of them were clearly for a heavy security door, two were for the street door, and there was one small key for the mailbox. I looked in the city guide and made a rather didactic map of the route I would have to take once I got off the 62 bus at the end of the line.

I didn't have to wait long for the bus, and I had no problem figuring out where I was going. I was not until I got to Via Pavia that it occurred to me that I should look around to see if I had been followed, if anyone was watching me. At the same moment, I remembered that I had forgotten my hat and that it was damp out. The idea that I might get an ear infection seemed more worrisome than the fear that I might have been followed.

I tried one of the keys, the street door opened and I walked across a small courtyard until I reached a glass-panel door that I opened with the other key. Nina's friend was named Corace and he lived on the third floor. I decided not to take the elevator, and took the stairs instead, but after walking up just a few steps, I walked back downstairs and, in keeping with my old habit of being helpful whenever I could, I went to the mailbox and took out a conspicuous number of letters and newsletters addressed to Corace.

The building was silent, dimly lit.

I walked upstairs. The security door opened just as easily as the downstairs doors. I left the door ajar so that I could see by the hall light to find the light switch. It was only when I flipped the switch on and nothing happened that I suddenly felt concerned. When Corace left town, he must have turned off the electricity. In the shadowy entryway, I saw on the wall to my right the handle of a cabinet. I pulled the cabinet open and found the master circuit breaker. Every room in the apartment lit up at once.

I closed the front door. I immediately went in search of the bookshelves, and in the living room I found an old set of built-in shelves that extended all the way up to the ceiling and covered every wall in the room, except for the wall that had two windows. The books were arranged rigorously in alphabetical order by author, so that there might be a gardening book next to a book by Diderot. I carefully leaned the aluminum ladder against the rail that ran along the cornice of the bookshelves, and climbed up to look under "b," on the highest shelves.

For some time, I had been suffering from a fear of falling. I could tell that my leg joints weren't as flexible as they used to be, and I moved increasingly cautiously as time went by. For at least ten years now, I walked downhill without skipping, without running, taking cautious short steps. On the bus, it was easy for me to lose my balance, and so I gripped the straps and the rails on the seats, but I still constantly bumped into other passengers, and had to beg pardon over and over. The discovery that my body wasn't what it used to be had failed to become an entrenched idea. I still occasionally forgot myself and moved as if I were a young man. It was like a dream that lasted for a few seconds: I'd walk a little faster, even run briefly, or leap over something that was in my way. But then my heart would begin pounding in my throat, I'd feel as if I were about to fall, and I'd remember my newfound caution. I'd ward off the memory of my youthful limbs, and remember to respect the body I had now.

I climbed carefully up the ladder, one rung at a time. When I came level with the topmost shelf, I turned to look out at the chandelier full of fake candles, dangling crystal pendants, the hexagonal tile floor, the top of the desk covered with all kinds of papers, the large television set, and the grey sofa on which lay no fewer than four remote controls. For a moment, I glimpsed myself perched up there, wearing my overcoat, in a stranger's apartment, gripping the top rung with both hands, knuckles white with strain. I turned grumpy, as if someone were making fun of me. I hastily rummaged through the books in search of Broch, but I soon found that *The Death of Virgil* wasn't there, and where it should have been there was a dark gaping hole shaped like an isosceles triangle.

That setback absorbed my full attention. I had expected the book to be in its proper place, a natural consequence of the fact that the city was Rome, there was such a street as Via Pavia, that a certain Corace really did live there, and that the keys fit the doors. I looked, I looked again: it was no good. I came back down the ladder a little too fast, forgetful of caution, and I was careless on the last two rungs. My left foot touched the floor, my right foot was too high, I lost my balance, and before I knew it I was flat on my back on the tile floor.

I lay there, motionless, the thud of my body hitting the ground echoing in my ears. I was disoriented.

Falling was something I was afraid of and therefore it hadn't happened to me for a long time. When was the last time I had fallen? Had I ever fallen so suddenly, so violently? The prudence, the caution that I had learned after turning fifty had made me forget that, even though you skin your knee, you sprain your ankle, you break your wrist, afterward the bones set and knit, the swelling goes down, the scab falls off, the body heals. I found myself quavering in fear, like a man unable to fall asleep after working hard all day long, because he is no longer confident he'll wake up in the morning.

Get up. I slowly rose, gasping with pain; I rubbed my back, bending first one leg then the other. No bones were broken. The house was silent again, after the noise of the fall. I put the ladder back where it had been, and the movement caused a slight spasm of pain in the middle of my back. What if the book was somewhere else? I ran my eyes over all the other shelves, even though, from where I stood, authors' names and book titles were so many dark blots. I seemed to remember that the cover of the old edition was yellow, but I might have been mistaken. Hadn't there been a new edition with a red cover? I picked out all the yellow covers and the red covers, but none of them looked like *The Death of Virgil*.

I thought of Nina. I convinced myself that she really hadn't asked me to do anything dangerous. She was a woman about to turn thirty, possibly involved in violent activities that demanded firm political convictions, military experience, ties to people inside and outside the country, a fervent adherence to everything that in every corner of the world was strongly opposed to quiet living and regular habits. Would a person of her kind ever think of making use of me, a sadly tattered denizen of precisely that world? She had sent me to get a book, and I had failed to find it. I hadn't been able to meet the challenge of climbing a ladder. I was ashamed of myself. I had grown so old that I had forgotten I was an old man, and I had come to believe that Nina was so naïve as to entrust me with a subversive mission.

Then I went into the bedroom.

It was a small room, with a double bed, lots of photographs on the walls, many of which, to judge from the clothing worn by the young women, and the young men with long hair and beards, dated from the Seventies. Had Corace been one of those young people, as the books in his library indicated? Or was he the son, much older now than his mother and father had been when those photographs were taken?

I noticed that there were lots of books piled high on one of the bedside tables. That was where I found *The Death of Virgil*. I flipped through the pages; they were covered with underlinings in pen, exclamation points, and the occasional question mark. I went to page 46; there only one phrase was underlined. It said: "Only falsehood wins renown, not understanding." I copied it onto a sheet of paper and left in a hurry.

4.

I decided to introduce a space after the phrase "subversive mission." I did it, not because I felt what we might call an aesthetic need, but rather because I wasn't really happy with the last few lines. I read them, I re-read them, I grew increasingly dissatisfied with them. For instance, the photographs on the walls from the Seventies struck me as a lazy detail; for instance, I wasn't sure that finding the book by Broch right away helped the plot; for instance, I wasn't certain about the quotation I had chosen. I wondered: why this phrase about falsehood, renown, understanding, instead of other more generic phrases, less complicated or perhaps more in keeping with the story's political theme? Wasn't there a risk that the concept might overlay the function of secret code that the quote was supposed to have and, in future developments of the story, make something that wasn't relevant at all seem supremely germane?

For a few days, I couldn't write at all. Instead I reread the three chapters, added some commas, removed others, modified an adjective here and there, cut out the passage that described life waiting beneath the city's asphalt, then I changed my mind and put it back in. I was constructing the story the way I usually do, reinventing my experience. The protagonist had been a teacher, just as I had, though I made him a little older than me. I had recently had a former student, but a young man, not a woman, who had been the subject, marginally and without justification, in a police investigation into the new Red Brigades, but I hadn't called him, I hadn't met with him. I had only exchanged a few words with his father, who'd been a friend of mine for decades. I wasn't a widower, my wife enjoyed excellent health, the only trait of hers I had utilized was her frequent irony about my excessive indulgence. I climbed up and down the aluminum ladder of our bookshelves at home, I had never fallen off the ladder, I thought I was in excellent shape, though I had recently decided to take a battery of exams, in the wake of an outburst of hypochondria; it had emerged that my triglyceride levels were quite elevated (419) and there was something wrong with my thyroid. I was the father of two daughters (I had a son as well), who, however, showed little or no interest in me and above all showed no concern whatever for my health. No one had ever asked me to go get a book in an apartment in Via Pavia or any other street in Rome, but once, thirty years ago, a colleague of mine named Luciano, a comrade, as we used to say back then, had asked me to go to the apartment of a girl that he had lived with and with whom he was now breaking up, to remove two suitcases crammed full of his belongings, a favor that I had performed for him even though, given my propensity to let my imagination roam free, I had entertained some suspicions and quite a bit of baseless anxiety. It is normal for me to construct a story in this manner, and it is normal that, when I oscillate between reality and fantasy, one day a story might seem real to me, while the next day the false aspect of the story overwhelms the true part, and I am suddenly unable to bring the story to completion. Thus, when I realized that little by little, doubt adding to doubt, my faith in the authenticity of the story was beginning to wane, I wasn't too worried, and decided to wait for the desire to write to return. If it didn't, too bad: for a while I'd be grumpy about it, but sooner or later I'd move on to another story.

One morning I received a phone call from an Italian publisher, Fandango Libri. They asked if I would be interested in taking part in a publishing project to raise money for the victims of the Indian Ocean tsunami. The idea was to add to the Italian translation of *New Beginnings*, a book put out by the London publisher Bloomsbury, the profits of which went to providing disaster relief after the devastating tsunami in southeast Asia; the Italian edition would include beginnings of stories that Italian writers were working on. Would I be willing to donate the first chapter of a novella or novel or screenplay that I was writing? I said that I would be happy to and went back to work on the first pages of *Claim for Damages*—that was the provisional title of my book—to get them into better shape and, in the meantime, understand if they were good enough to be printed. But almost without realizing it, I soon found myself wondering not whether the short story was good, but whether I was good: I, the man writing the story, I the man fine-tuning the sentences on behalf of charity. At first, I asked myself the question in a generic manner, casting back my memory to the times when I had been told I was a good little boy, a well-behaved student, a good young man, a good man, a good person. Then I thought it over in a more analytical manner and concluded that I had always had within me, ever since I was quite small, a violence that was constantly on the verge of exploding, a lust for mayhem that I had learned quite young to repress, keeping tamped down my feelings of rage, my aggressive instincts, my treachery, my evil. In other words, if I was good, I was good only in the sense that I had succeeded in imprisoning my inborn ferocity.

When had I tamed myself? It had been a lengthy apprenticeship, begun when I was as young as ten, and continued relentlessly throughout my adolescence, when I had discovered to my own terror that I wanted to murder somebody: my father, a sarcastic friend, my professor of Latin and Greek, even a rude passerby. It was not until I was almost twenty that I began to suspect that, along with the repression of my violent impulses, I had repressed everything, even my ability to experience a profound emotion, even my impulse to do good deeds and help others. I had become as good as I had hoped to be, but good with the cautious detachment of one who never indulge in excess.

In fact, I had no enthusiastic and generous impulses. Once—I was still in high school, it was 1960, 1961—I was out walking with a friend of mine named Furio. We hadn't yet become involved in politics, we weren't really involved in anything. We saw a crowd of people in Piazza Garibaldi, sitting in silence on the pavement, with the station behind them: a small group of men, no women; they hadn't shaven in days, their faces white and violet. They were enclosed behind a sort of corral of signs saying we've been fired, we're hungry, our children are hungry, help us, support our struggle. That was the first time I ever really noticed factory workers. Laid-off factory workers. But the only emotion I felt then was a mixture of repulsion at their desperate poverty and hunger and a hatred—real hatred, a plunge into the red, murky depths of the chest—for the ill-defined silhouettes of those who had tossed them out into the street.

I recall thinking quite distinctly that they had really been tossed into the street. It didn't seem like a manner of speech, it really was the vile and filthy street around the central station of Naples, and I recoiled, in fear and indignation. But my friend, Furio, had a very different reaction. He asked me to give him all the money I had in my pocket, he added it to his own money, and he ran off without a word of explanation. He returned a short while later, with liters of milk in a large cardboard box, stepped through the enclosure of signs, and handed it over to the protesting workers. He had translated a feeling into a generous gesture, useful in the here and now. I had restrained myself, and I had done nothing.

This then was the point. Perhaps, in those difficult years, I had taken care only to avoid becoming vicious and, completely absorbed in that effort, I had transformed myself into a sage young man, or at least I had learned to behave like one. Sage, in Italian, *savio*, was a fine adjective that I had always liked, even as early as elementary school, when I had first heard it with devout admiration in the surname of Domenico Savio, the young boy who, under the guidance of Don Bosco, had taken the path of first blessedness and later, saintliness. It had been—I thought this while I worked, obsessively, for days and days on the beginning of the story, and I was already planning to dig deeper into the restrained, compressed nature of the protagonist, perhaps by introducing the episode of the laid-off factory workers—it had been this training to become sage and wise that had turned me into a upstanding person.

5

I decided to send only the first two chapters to Fandango Libri; I still had some doubts about the third chapter. I called the editorial director, Rosaria Carpinelli. She said with great professional courtesy that she was eager to learn how the story of the elderly professor would end, and praised the passage: "I had grown old doing not what I genuinely wanted to do, but rather the things that fit in with the way I saw myself." This—I have to say—restored my desire to finish the story: sometimes all it takes is a small encouragement to push you to sit down at your desk and continue your work with new hope. But since I had a lot of work for the movies in that period, I was obliged to write in my head, the way I do when I am chasing after a story without having time to devote to composing it on the page.

I imagined that the elderly professor had left the apartment in Via Pavia without finding *The Death of Virgil.* Now he took the bus back home, and he was starting to feel some pain from his fall, especially up high, between his shoulder blades. As he walked through the main street door into his apartment building, the concierge stepped out of his little cubicle and told him, with a hint of ill-concealed satisfaction, that a policeman had come by looking for him, and had left an envelope for him. The professor opened the envelope and discovered that he had been summoned for an interview the following morning, at nine o'clock, at the local police station. Of course, he didn't sleep a wink all night, wondering what he should do, scheming how to alert Nina, but then fearing that he would only complicate matters (he might be followed, the line might be tapped) decided to do nothing. Nonetheless, the next morning, he showed up at the police station near his home, and was received by an inspector a little older than forty, closely shaven, nearly bald, and exceedingly courteous. The dialogue must have gone something like this:

"Take a good look, Professor: do you remember me?"

"I couldn't say, do we know one another?"

"Look at me carefully."

"I'm sorry, I can't say that I know you."

"It's me, Sellitto."

"Sellitto?"

"That's right, Professor, Augusto Sellitto!"

"Sellitto, *caro*, *carissimo*, how are you?"

I went on like this for days, turning phrases over in my head, weighing them to see if they were natural and if they sounded good.

I had been in a police station only a few times in my life, to renew my passport and to report the theft (or loss) of my wallet. I had no experience with the police, I didn't even know if there was a specific protocol for summoning someone to come in for an interview. I was feeling my way, combining my own minor experiences with images I'd seen in movies or on television. I promised myself that I'd decide on details later, when I was done writing, details like how exactly one finds oneself face to face with a cop. Now I was interested only in identifying the proper tone with which to introduce into the story another former student, this Sellitto, a police inspector, without having the meeting seem contrived.

My students have become everything imaginable: doctors, postmen, travel agents, night porters, bankers, teachers, airline hostesses, the jobless, writers, journalists, and singers. I've had a fair number of students who have become policemen, so the idea was plausible. One of them was a lovely woman with whom I had once gone to eat a pizza and talk about her love life: on that occasion I had glimpsed her pistol in her open pocketbook, and it had made an impression on me; it seemed inconceivable that an awkward young girl who once blushed easily should now go around armed, even when she was off duty. Another one of my students had come to see me at school, about fifteen years go, to tell me that he was in DIGOS, the anti-terrorism and special operations branch of the intelligence services, and to complain that things were going badly, that he was forced to see things in his work (he wouldn't say what) that contrasted with the things that I had taught him. I wanted to construct the character of the police inspector out of those former students of mine. I imagined that the retired professor would at first feel he was in danger and leave his apartment out of anxiety, walking laboriously, irritated by the pain in his back and by everything that had happened; that he would then go to see the inspector in a state of tension that would be difficult to conceal; and that he would finally feel a sense of relief and growing euphoria at his impression that he exerted an old and solid authority over the very person from whom, until a moment previous, he had had so much to fear.

The idea, of course, was to present the main character with two different products of his work as a teacher, a female former student who was under investigation for armed conspiracy, and a male former student, who was now a member of the police force, involved in an investigation of the new Red Brigades. I worked up a dialogue that went roughly like this:

"Yesterday morning I took a look at a report on my desk, and what did I see? I saw your name: Professor Domenico Stasi. And when I did, I said to myself, that's my teacher from high school, and now here we are."

"I'm happy to see you again."

"How long has it been? I'm forty-five now; let's say that I was sixteen when you came into our classroom for the first time: it's been no fewer than twenty-eight years."

"Twenty-nine."

"Sure, that's right, twenty-nine, I never was very good at arithmetic."

"As far as I can recall, you were never very good at Italian either."

"But I always enjoyed your lessons. I remember the time you read us the Novella of the Fat Woodcutter like it was yesterday."

"You remember the story of the Fat Woodcutter from the *Decameron*?"

"Sure, we even argued about it."

"You and me?"

"In front of the whole class."

"And what did we argue about?"

"About the prank that Filippo Brunelleschi played on the Fat Woodcutter. I said that it took a special kind of genius to convince someone that he is not himself but someone else."

"And what did I say?"

"You shook your head every so often: it was clear you disagreed."

"I was on the Fat Woodcutter's side and against Brunelleschi?"

"Now, that I couldn't say, but I do remember that you said: 'Sellitto, staying oneself for an entire lifetime is such a difficult challenge, that if someone manages to persuade you that you are no longer Sellitto but, let us say, Stasi, well, that person may be a minor genius but he's not someone I respect. No, that person has behaved unjustly.'"

"I said that?"

"Sure. You used to come out with things that no one else could ever have thought up. What's this?, I said to myself, the professor is defending an idiot like the Fat Woodcutter against Filippo Brunelleschi? I liked you for that."

"I did what I could, Sellitto. In any case, thanks very much, I'm glad you remember me fondly."

"Fondly is too lukewarm, Professor. You were capable of showing us injustice in just about anything, even things we never normally thought about. I remember when you told us that injustice begins even before you're born, with the combination of chromosomes, such as for instance when you wind up with genes that make you ugly instead of handsome."

"I said that?"

"You said that and more. For instance, you said that another great underlying injustice is the difference in people's intelligence."

"I don't remember that."

"But I do. You would get pretty heated, you'd say this sort of thing and get really mad. There was a tension, in class, and I would wonder: if you're born poor, then you can blame the rich; but if you're born ugly and stupid, who do you blame? Why doesn't the professor resign himself to the way things are? Why does he get so mad?"

"We professors say some real nonsense in the classroom. Outside we tend to restrain ourselves a little more, but in class we tend to lose our inhibitions."

"It never seemed like nonsense, it really never did. Quite the opposite. You had a clear objective, if you ask me. You wanted to help us grow up angry. Once you even said it to me. You said: Sellitto, you're too indulgent, you need to get angry."

"What did you say?"

"Me? I said: 'Even if I get angry, Professor, what does that change?' And you replied: 'Go ahead and get angry, and then let me know.'"

"And did you get angry?"

"No. But I have to say I agree with you: it's an injustice

that I am the way I am, short, fat, and look here, practically bald."

"You're a likable fellow."

"No, I'm an ugly fellow, and not a very smart one. If I were otherwise, I'd have picked another line of work. Instead, here I am, surrounded by all these dusty old files, and just ten minutes ago, while I was waiting for you to come in, I was saying to myself: the professor taught me to recognize all forms of injustice and to get angry, but what do I do instead? I put in jail those very people who battle so ferociously against injustice that they break the law and become criminals."

"If someone commits a crime, they should be punished: the work you do is necessary, Sellitto."

"But you pushed us to commit crimes."

"I don't understand."

"You used to say: don't be indulgent, get angry, seize justice for yourselves and for others."

"But pushing someone to demand justice isn't pushing them to commit crimes."

"Crimes, Professor, if you examine them closely, are the product of a burning rage against injustice."

"Now that's an exaggeration."

"But you said it, Professor; I still have my notes. Once you explained to us that the worst and most horrifying injustices are the ones that are protected by the law. 'In these cases,' you told us, 'there is no possibility of justice, unless you leave the realm of legality.'"

"I rule out the possibility that I ever said anything of the sort, Sellitto."

"I couldn't say, but I remember it. And anyway I have proof that you have a soft spot for those who break the law in the name of justice. For instance, just yesterday morning you met Antonia Villa, your former student, under investigation for armed conspiracy. You met her—here it is—in a café in Talenti.

"When I read that, in the report, I admit I was a little jealous. This young lady, who may very well have committed a series of horrible crimes, got in touch with you and you honored her with a lengthy conversation. But you never came looking for me, in fact you didn't even recognize me at first, and I still suspect that you pretended to remember me just to keep from hurting my feelings, and that in reality all I am to you is a black hole, nothing. What was this Antonia Villa like as a girl? Pretty? A rebel? Did she get angry and demand justice even though the law protected injustice?"

I went on like this for quite a while. I worked on the dialogue in the evening, before going to sleep, or in the early morning, on the bus, in the metro, on the train. In my mind, I could hear the voices of the professor and his former student, the policeman. As soon as the dialogue struck me as plausible, I tried writing it out. Seeing them in writing, however, only impoverished the voices I had just rehearsed. In my mind they sounded real, but as soon as I wrote them down, the imagined speech became mannered. Above all, I had no time, in that phase of the composition, to come up with anything more than a hasty set of notes.

"Professor, teach me how to think."

"I already tried, Sellitto."

"No, what I mean is: what opinion should a person have about the war in Iraq? Bush was right to kick out Saddam Hussein but he was wrong to start the war? Is that correct?"

"It was up to the Iraqis—not the president of the United States—to get rid of Saddam."

"But if an oppressed people needs a little help, should we give it to them or not?"

"Sure. But not by flattening the country with a rain of bombs and going in to occupy their country with an army of ignorant, ferocious torturers."

"Then how?"

"For instance, by supporting the right to rebellion. But that's a right that governments around the world fear like the plague. They prefer armies, wars, and the secret police."

"And do democratic societies fear this right as well?"

"They fear it more than any other society, especially if the rituals of democracy are in fact a rigged game."

"And what about Israel, Professor, what can we say about Israel? Are we on the side of the Jews or against the Jews?"

"Israel is a country, Sellitto, not a people. If a state has a bad policy, it should be criticized and opposed, Jewish or non-Jewish."

"But you hammered our balls for months and months about the fact that anti-Semitism is always lurking in the shadows, don't you remember?"

"Sellitto, if I criticize the politics of the French state, am I attacking French culture? If I criticize the policies of the Vatican, does that make me anti-Catholic? French culture has nothing to do with it, Catholicism has nothing to do with it, the Muslims, the Buddhists, and even the Jews have nothing to do with it. A state is a territory, a government, and an army."

"A people!"

"I don't know if a state is a people."

"Of course it is, how can you say that? I studied it."

"I don't even know if there is such a thing as a people, Sellitto."

"Professor, then what are we?"

"Exploiters and the exploited, the oppressed and their oppressors."

I imagined an abstractly didactic tone of voice. I planned to rehearse all the problems of the planet, situating Professor Stasi somewhere between the polite indifference of the elderly and an ill-concealed extremism, rooted in his long-ago youth if not in his very nature, in an obscure need for the paradoxical, in an obsession with radical concepts.

It was in search of this extremism that I was rummaging through my memory. I remembered how once, when I was young, I had signed a petition, during the Six Day War, against Israel. It was 1967, that's right. I felt sure, at the time, that I was doing the right thing and yet I felt confused, unhappy with myself. I had discovered the vital necessity of political involvement, between the end of the Fifties and the early Sixties, reading a book about the Holocaust; it cited statistics, and documented them with horrible, intolerable photographs. What then should I do? I loved the Jews and I was militating on behalf of the Arab states? I was declaring that I was in favor of the destruction of Israel, bridgehead of Yankee imperialism, and yet I would have been willing to fight to the last drop of blood against the Nazis and the Fascists? That was the beginning of a long and perplexing conundrum. Then, four years later, I read *Portnoy's Complaint*, and I thoroughly enjoyed it and found it funny. But, good Lord, every time I smiled, every time I laughed, I felt as if I were doing wrong. Wasn't it true that this book could just as easily have warmed the cockles of Joseph Goebbels's heart? So what was I doing? Was I harboring anti-Semitic prejudices? Was I laughing at Mr. Portnoy, Mrs. Portnoy, and the habits and customs of the little Yiddish family described by the ungrateful Alex Portnoy? Was I laughing at the Jews? And so on. I wanted to search back through contradictory moments of my youth: what was I thinking, why did I sign the petition, what were the surface reasons and the subterranean reasons. I wanted to gather material with which to narrate the emotional confusion, the movement involved in subscribing to violence in the name of Justice. Israel should be driven into the sea. And so? Should we slaughter the prosperous, well-armed Israelis, who were slaughtering the emaciated Palestinians, similar in so many ways to the skinny street urchins, the *scugnizzi,* of my own city? Who was doing wrong to whom? What's the correct point of view? What is the proper mode? I wanted an account of the terrifying need for bloody action that exploded into the world unexpectedly, apparently inevitably, from within a judicious lexicon of thoughts and words, from deep inside a cautious and considered assessment of the points of views of all the various parties involved.

This is how I was planning Stasi. He is incapable—I thought—of understanding the wisdom of a middle road, but he's not just an hysterical old man, he's well educated, he sets forth extreme theories in a balanced, judicious tone. Once, I tried to sketch out a sort of thumbnail portrait. The professor was thinking back, perhaps as a result of his conversations with Sellitto, to the lives squandered, the workers murdered by sub-human working conditions in exchange for the pennies of their miserable salaries, the protesters mown down by the police in the streets during demonstrations, the bodies blown to bits in state-sponsored terrorist attacks, those killed by the neo-fascist revival of men claiming to operate in the name of Providence, and he saw—I focused greedily on this image—a rivulet of blood running from one end of Italy to the other, throughout the planet, the years of his life as a sort of chart of the hatred that, if you studied it, only demanded more and more blood, immediately. I wonder, he said to himself, whether there's a list broken down by category: so many manual laborers murdered, so many factory workers, so many policemen, so many businessmen, so many magistrates, so many dentists, so many plumbers, so many criminals, so many professors, so many students. He had muddled through the decades of unbridled furies working quietly as a teacher, he had never changed jobs. Many of his pupils had wonderful memories of him, they'd call him up, wishing him a happy birthday every year. His radical beliefs had always been considered a form of mental honesty. His own life story was first and foremost a history of the books he had read, and he eagerly recounted that story to himself, often with a note of self-deprecation. At the end of the Fifties, he was a young man filled with admiration for those who helped the poor and the oppressed; he wanted to live his life in keeping with the words of the Gospels. Then he had made new friends, and had engaged in long discussions, and he had come to the conclusion that Christian charity was complicit with the oppressors, and that it was necessary to side with the proletariat and abolish private ownership of the means of production. For a while he had struggled mightily to resolve the issue of violence. Subsequently he had decided, but without emphasis— Stasi detested the overemphatic—that the violence being implemented against the proletariat was so overwhelming that it would be impossible to obtain any real change without taking up arms. And so he set about his studies with a view to preparing for the revolution with both words and action, and in the meanwhile worked to become a new man, courteous but determined, scornful toward the strong, cordial with the weak. In the early Sixties he became a member of the PCI, the Italian Communist Party, even though he disapproved of its politics, even though he despised the USSR, even though he had read Trotsky, even though he knew all about Stalin's crimes. Nonetheless, the PCI was the workers' party and he felt that he was *operaista*—pro-worker. He had begun teaching in 1964, and he had participated in the first anti-war demonstrations against the US involvement in Vietnam. It had been a happy time, during which it seemed to him that being a member of a group of comrades carrying on the struggle defined him better, energized his body and his mind. When the student revolt finally exploded, it struck him as a petty bourgeois uprising without a future. Still, he had subscribed enthusiastically to the idea that world revolution was at the gates, and he had resigned his membership in the Italian Communist Party. The feeling of fullness had only grown. Marching through the crowded streets with so many others in protest marches, crowding into rooms and lecture halls filled with comrades, helped to make you feel more like yourself. Then came rigid affiliations and factions, the demands for credentials. That was when Stasi began to feel uncomfortable. He had never cared much for Mao's China. He had developed some enthusiasm for Cuba, for Che Guevara, but tepid enthusiasm, at best. He had always felt revulsion for uniforms, including the uniforms worn by revolutionaries. He felt annoyance with leaders, he had never agreed with those who considered themselves—or were considered by others—to be The Best, the Great Helmsman, or other capitalized monikers. Instead, he had a distinct predilection for those who wished to abolish hierarchies: no delegates, direct democracy, power to the working class. Nothing, in his view, was as urgent and decisive as a rally. His speeches, during the course of the feverish, overwhelming Seventies, were widely appreciated for their forthright, unabashed clarity and, at the same time, as if by a miracle, for their courteous tone. On more than one occasion, he had been offered positions and responsibilities, though those offers were made with the understanding that he would either reject the offer, or else that he would bring such dedication and rigor to these offices that soon he would be forced to resign and make way for others. In the end, the impassioned, furious turbulence of those years paled into a drab routine, a series of mechanical gestures. What his generation had undertaken, in every sector of civil society, had been left half-completed, a Tower of Babel interrupted during construction, scaffolding either reused for other purposes or, more often, swallowed up by the old landscape. Stasi, at the turn of the Eighties, felt the need to devote himself more and more to reading, to study, in an attempt to understand what was happening all around him, but he had never given up his habit, when the occasion presented itself, of raising his hand in public, of speaking in tones of harsh and well informed criticism. Even now that his body was in sharp decline, he continued to be swept by a wave of acutely reasoned, incisive indignation at the terrible and despicable direction of the entire planet, a wave that was as much a part of his nature as would have been if he were still a tousle-haired young man. But the only ones who heard his outbursts nowadays were the members of the block association and the supporters of a committee that he himself had founded to protect moderately green green space a short walk from his home.

I went on like this, writing rapidly, but soon I was bored. I was slipping into the generic. If I wanted to do a good job, I needed to cite parties, splinter groups, magazines, newspapers, political leaders, intellectuals, street demonstrations, books from the period. But that type of diligent execution wasn't the work I loved, it struck me as a scholastic exercise, I preferred concise formulations such as: "The only acts of which the professor felt he was capable were linguistic in nature—I advise you to, I promise you that—and those too, throughout the course of his life, had almost always proven ineffectual." And so I returned to the dialogue between Sellitto and Stasi. I let it echo in my mind without "he said," "he asked," he "added," "shot back," or "replied": a stack of imagined phrases in quotes.

"Where is history heading, Professor?"

"Nowhere, Sellitto. What happens happens, and that's all."

"Then it's just a pointless mess."

"Yes, I'm afraid that's correct."

"But once you told us that there's always one side that is in the right and the other side is in the wrong."

"Well, that's true."

"But the pointless mess can't clean itself up."

"Not for now."

"Then what?"

"Then we need to make choices, just like always: either you work to achieve paradise on earth, or else you're working on behalf of the inferno."

"And you're in favor of paradise?"

"Sure. There are too many people who live in the inferno, and that's not acceptable."

"Still a Communist, eh?"

"I believe I am."

"But you had us read *One Day in the Life of Ivan Denisovich.*"

"And so? Allow me to recommend that you read *Kolyma Tales.* And *The Stones Cry Out: A Cambodian Childhood, 1975-1980.*"

"Those were horrifying books, too?"

"Yes."

"You're an odd duck, Professor. If you know these things, why do you continue to hope for paradise on earth?"

"It's not that I hope for it, it's a necessity."

"But an intermediate solution, you rule that out, Professor? A balanced world, with a mixed salad of paradise and inferno, what do you say, would you settle for that?"

"What can I say, Sellitto? The work you do ought to teach you more things than I can ever hope to. You know better than I do what the inferno is like."

Et cetera, et cetera. But I wasn't satisfied, I had something else in mind, a deeper, darker secret that refused to emerge, to bob to the surface.

6

One day I happened to be on a bus; I was on my way to RAI state television headquarters to discuss a script that, at first, had been approved, only to be rejected, worked on, and finally rejected again, all depending on the see-sawing moods and waves of terror that filled the working lives of assistants, directors, and government bureaucrats.

I rarely take taxis, I don't drive a Vespa or a moped, and I haven't driven a car in the city for at least ten years: I am one of the few well-to-do Italians who still uses public transportation, buses that are generally crowded with tourists, poor people, madmen, purse-snatchers, and immigrants. I climbed aboard the 495 bus, but I didn't even have time to look around for a seat. A fifty-year-old man began to insult a very fat black woman who, in his opinion, had shoved him while trying to make her way down the aisle. He reeled off a succession of crude and offensive phrases, and then started in on anybody that came under the heading of non-European or migrant or any other epithet you care to name. I could sense a swelling surge of rage in my veins, the fury of an old man with clogged arteries. No matter how much I told myself to calm down, the blood was rushing to my temples and I didn't know how to rein in my temper.

It's an awkward condition to have, but it's part of my nature. Generally, I try to be like the Zen monk who, when accused by a young girl of being the father of her child, breaks his silence only to say, "Is that so?" and then unprotestingly takes care of the newborn infant. Then, months later, when the girl confesses that the real father was a young man passing through the village, the monk again says: "Is that so?" and continues taking care of the baby. In other words, I do my best, and I've always done my best, all my life, to be capable of saying "Is that so?" in every circumstance, and on the whole, I've been successful. "Is that so? Is that so? Is that so?" But I know that each time I narrowly resisted the impulse to turn violent; I have no real gift for impassivity. If I cross the threshold of silence, then it's as if I've been blinded by a red light, a warning light pushing me down paths from which there is no turning back. And so I said to the man: "Shut your mouth, you idiot."

"What the fuck do you want?"

"You need to apologize to the lady."

"And you need to go fuck yourself."

"No, you need to go fuck yourself, and fuck your mother and your sister too, you piece of shit. Get out of this bus and say the things you said to that poor woman to me, on the sidewalk. Let's go!"

I realized that I was already pushing him toward the exit door, I wanted to hurl him out onto the sidewalk the second the doors whooshed open and then rush down the steps and grip him furiously by the throat and throttle him until his eyes bulged out of their sockets. I had forgotten who I was, how old I was. Suddenly I was speaking in dialect, a turgid violent Neapolitan. It never entered my mind for a second that the other man could much more easily have done to me what I so urgently needed to do to him. On the contrary, I felt as if I were a furious, disembodied demon. I was certain that even if the man had stabbed me through and through, or shot me in the chest, I would have felt nothing, the only thing I understood was the blinding need to kill him.

He must have seen that burning need in my eyes, in the determination with which I pushed him toward the exit, in the fury in my hands. He muttered something—said that I was an old man, so he'd let me live this once. He stepped out of the bus the instant the doors swung open, and I stepped down behind him, I didn't waste a second, but I still couldn't lay my hands on him. He had turned white as a sheet, he was stepping away from me, walking backwards with footsteps that were alternately clumsy and frantic, his mouth was gaping and closing. He didn't escape immediately, but it struck me that in order to get away from me, he was gathering himself together—collecting himself—with all his strength and then splintering himself away heavily, now a leg, now an arm, now the head. It was a weird, off-kilter flight: he hastened away, but uncomfortably, uneasily. However it happened, he was soon gone.

My rage subsided slowly, I could hear myself wheezing. I sensed my temples pounding. Before, I hadn't even been aware I had a heart, and now it had swollen in my chest, and it was violently thrashing against my throat. I leaned against a plane tree, and I saw the pure madness of my reaction. When I returned home, after my meeting at the RAI headquarters in Viale Mazzini, I was suddenly very weak, I said nothing to my wife, I went to sleep for a while. I was exhausted as if I had run uphill, and I slept deeply.

When I reawakened, I worked for a couple of hours, I jotted down some notes. Ever since the memory had resurfaced of Comrade Luciano—that is, the young man, the boy (though back then we felt sure that we were hard-bitten, experienced adults) for whom thirty years ago I had gone to pick up a pair of suitcases—I had been eager to fit him into the story of Stasi, somehow. I pulled out an old metal strongbox in which I kept photographs from my years as a professor, and I looked for pictures of myself with Luciano. In one old picture, I had an arm draped over his shoulders, I had a pitch-black beard, I looked a little puffy, and he wore his hair long, almost down to his shoulders, and he had a contented expression on his face. In another picture, we were with our students, the entire graduating class. They were all giving the clenched-fist salute, boys and girls. Luciano, in their midst, was raising his left hand clenched in a fist, with a warm smile. I wasn't, I was tucked out of sight, I was always embarrassed, even then, about clenched fists, shouted slogans, spectacular behavior. I also found a photograph of myself with Nadia, Luciano's lover, to whose apartment I had gone to pick up the suitcases, though in this photograph they might not have gotten together yet. She was trying on a floppy hat outside of a junk shop, perhaps we were on a field trip. She wasn't as pretty as I remembered her. She looked somewhat moonfaced. She wore a pleated skirt, a turtleneck, and over the turtleneck, a white blouse. I wanted to use those photographs to establish the story of the suitcases. We were all colleagues, fellow-professors—Luciano, Nadia, and I. We taught kids from the same year, the same kids in various classes. One day Luciano had shown up at school looking dead beat, like he hadn't slept a wink; he was wearing the same shirt he'd worn the day before.

"What's happening?"

"I can't take it anymore, I can't stand her."

"Why do you keep fighting? If it's over, it's over."

"Can I ask you to do me a favor?"

I thought back to that day, I focused, studying the photographs. Luciano had a big, droopy mustache, bright lively eyes, always a little bloodshot, the skin on his face mottled. His laughter was highly infectious. He even laughed when he was angry, and he raised a knuckly fist, his eyes wide open. He laughed, he'd wave his arms in the air, shout, and become violent, then he'd become all brotherly love again, in the space of a few minutes. He smoked Italian-made MS cigarettes, without filters, alternating them with equally vile Gauloises. He had a special gift for the piano, but he kept it to himself, it irritated him if anyone mentioned it. Once he had allowed me—me alone—to listen in secret, from a corner, while he played Chopin. It was clearly a great love of his, his fingers brushed the ivories with carefully modulated gestures; he struck me as a good player but no prodigy. He understood my opinion immediately and stopped playing abruptly, becoming the chaotic noisy man he was usually, and turned the conversation to politics and sex. He had a way of communicating with women that allowed him, in the space of a brief informal conversation, to venture well within the normal comfort zone of personal space. Girls threw their arms open to him as if they were automatic doors, they quickly felt at ease with him. They grazed him, they touched him, they tucked themselves under his arms, they said things and did things as if they'd known him for decades and implicitly trusted him.

Nadia, for instance, had decided in the space of a single week to leave her husband and go live with Luciano. She was petite—half his size, which was considerable—and was slender, with close-cropped hair, and lively glittering eyes (at least that was the impression I had at the time). As soon as they met, when she showed up as a substitute teacher, they started bantering playfully. They tossed insults back and forth, amidst laughter and insults that in a different relationship would surely have led to gasps and slaps and fisticuffs and scratched faces. The two of them, however, talked that way out of friendship, out of desire. At first, she seemed very stand-offish, but in the course of a few hours she abandoned all restraint, became mocking, and even pronounced a few giggling obscenities. One morning she knelt before him and wrapped her arms around his left leg, eyes misty, in the teacher's lounge, in full view of all the others. Later, in my car, I was at the wheel, a female friend of mine was in the passenger seat, Luciano and Nadia were in the back seat. I looked in the rearview mirror and noticed that they were shoving and elbowing one another with amusement, slapping each other lovingly. At a certain point, he grabbed her, turned her over his knee, belly down, and pulled down her jeans and panties, spanking her sharply, ferociously.

By the time a few months had passed, however, the laughter was gone, along with the desire in their fingers and their lips. Everything was consumed, and they had begun to quarrel viciously about politics or—so to speak—revolutionary ethics. She was a daughter of the petty bourgeoisie, interested only in romantic love, long drawn-out kisses: in bed, Luciano told me, she was very inhibited. Her husband? A spongy, whiny creature. But she couldn't seem to make up her mind to leave him, she was guilt-ridden, and she would return from time to time to the connubial residence. Do me a favor, he asked me, could you go pick up those suitcases, because if I go I'll just punch her in the face.

It was April, 1976. The apartment was on Via Pavia. I went there one afternoon, right after school let out. I took the elevator upstairs, passing floor after floor, but in the meantime I started to think: what do I really know about Luciano, what do I know about Nadia? No question, he is certainly a trusted comrade, but who knows about her. Maybe she tricked him into transporting something secret, her bourgeois air strikes me as a pretty good cover. Maybe she's involved in the armed struggle, maybe she's an undercover agent infiltrating the movement, they're only pretending to squabble; and for that matter, what do I really know about Luciano, we're all comrades, but there are different kinds of comrades; what kind of mess am I getting into here?

I knocked on the door. Nadia opened it, her eyes red with tears.

"Did you talk to him?"

"Yes."

"Did he tell you?"

I nodded yes. I noticed that she had a black mark on her chin, perhaps she had touched her chin with makeup-stained fingers.

"If he wants to come back, tell him okay, but he needs to stop treating me like a side of beef."

"He wants the suitcases."

She grimaced angrily and sniffed. She had them ready in the hallway, and she shoved them toward me with her foot, one after the other, and without a word shut the door.

I walked out into the street, overbalancing to one side from the weight of the suitcases: the one in my right hand was heavier than the bag in my left hand. I remember that there was a faint warm breeze. I took a bus, and then I took another bus. I felt a swelling doubt that this was all a sham. Her tears were a sham, her words were counterfeit. What am I transporting? I wondered, uneasily. Deep down, though, I was pleased with the situation. The condition of the working class. The proletariat enslaved by the bourgeoisie and their machinery. The toxins from the painting sector, the deafening thumps of the punch presses, pounding the steel plate and oozing grease, making the floors tremble. Society's collective wealth, deplorably in the hands of a privileged few. The illiterates of the world, crushed, forced to live hopeless lives in houses made of mud, while the bureaucracies of corrupt regimes lived the good life. The Communist revolution defiled by the unseemly haste to establish it in a single nation. Indignant thoughts. This filthy Italian bourgeoisie, with its governmental coterie of Mafia-affiliated profit-mongers. Begin the insurgency. Abandon words. Feel the handles of the suitcases as if they weren't called handles, but had no name, were nothing but pure physical contact of flesh against plastic, an electrochemical flow that reaches the brain and only there begins to trigger words. I am here. I am acting on behalf of a just cause. Apocalypse, Judgment, Resurrection. I walked slowly, heavily, my hands aching from the weight of the suitcases. I reached my apartment drenched in sweat, with an overwhelming sense of nausea.

How should I act? Take the suitcases to Luciano, shake hands, leave. Take the suitcases to Luciano, question him, ask him to let me look inside. Open them before going to his house, now, on the kitchen table. Rummage through them, find out what I was really transporting. Underwear, an AK-47, a bomb, plastic explosives, blasting caps. I'm not the sort of person that lets himself be used, I thought, I want to decide for myself. Say, freely: all right, I'll do it; or: no, I absolutely refuse. I opened the first suitcase. There were all sorts of things. Sweaters, socks, underwear, a safety razor, a bar of soap, a toothbrush, an espresso pot, a bedside lamp, a flashlight, a pair of pliers, a hammer, a box of nails. I opened the second suitcase: a pair of trousers, an overcoat, a nail clipper, two boxes of spaghetti, a camera, three pairs of blue jeans, a stack of folded shirts, all with a checkered pattern, and,

in the bottom of the suitcase, two pistols, a box of ammunition

I stopped there, I didn't even add a period, I just isolated that line: space above it, another space below it.

I stepped nervously away from the desk, I went over to the window. What kind of pistols? What caliber bullets? I'd gone too far, it wasn't ringing true. The pistols, the box of bullets. You read about these things in books, you saw them in movies, but in Luciano's suitcases, almost thirty years ago, I didn't find them. Now, if I wanted to put them in, to adapt that episode from my own life to the story of Stasi, no one could keep me from doing it, but I would need to make the decision to write exactly that type of story. In that case, I would set aside what truly belonged to me (the school, Luciano, Nadia, their affair in the mid-Seventies, the breakup, the suitcases) and I would just start inventing things, steering full tilt—or at least, once I'd read up on brands of firearms, calibers of bullets—into action scenes, with plenty of blood, with the pacing of a thriller, cops, terrorists, and the usual obscure plot involving the intelligence services. Perhaps, in order to work more effectively, I should go to the library, check the newspapers of the era, track down a forgotten episode from the news of the time, pilfer plot and details from the news stories. Perhaps I should get in touch with some of my magistrate friends, ask them to make copies of old trial records, depositions full of dialogue, targets, the unfolding of events, and skillfully convert them into a novel worthy of contemporary Italian writer, or at least one of the recent past. It is so absurd—this determination only to write about what I know directly, this stubborn limitation of the imagination. I erased from before my eyes written words, microfilms of old newspapers, the ghosts of Domenico Stasi and his former students, and I clearly saw the asphalt outside my apartment window, and the traffic.

I looked out the window with a start.

On the sidewalk across the street was the racist from the bus. I thought I recognized him, he was leaning against a white Renault Clio, and he was reading one of those giveaway newspapers.

I stepped quickly away from the window, holding my breath, as if the man across the street could hear me panting. Was it him, was it someone else? I took my digital camera out of my desk drawer and tiptoed cautiously over to the window again. I pulled back the curtain, and I snapped a couple of photographs. As if the man could hear the whirr of the camera, he looked up from his newspaper, stared for a few seconds at some random point on the building, and then went back to reading. I withdrew into the room. I took a look at the photos in the camera display, enlarged them until I could clearly see his face. No, perhaps it really wasn't the man I'd fought with. They resembled one another, that much was certain, they had a similar build; but the man on the screen was younger, perhaps by fifteen or twenty years. Or maybe not: maybe it's just that when you look at a person in a fit of rage you see them differently from when you look at them without that curtain of blood-red fury before your eyes.

I went back to the window, I leaned forward cautiously. The man was gone. I was tempted to download the pictures into the computer so that I could examine them more carefully, but I decided not to, I knew that I'd waste the rest of the afternoon. Instead I went back to writing; that little episode was starting to act as a stimulant. At first, I had a hard time sitting still; I wanted to get up and see if the man had come back, if he was there specifically to keep an eye on the street door of my apartment building. Then, the image of Stasi prevailed over everything else, his charcoal-grey Loden overcoat, his old-man's hat.

7

The professor left the police station in a calmer state of mind than that in which he had entered. Sellitto, he thought to himself, could not have any persecutorial intentions. He had become a police inspector thanks to Stasi's own lessons, and he seemed to be doing his job as if the sole foundation of everything he did were the words with which Stasi had taught him Italian literature and history, the basic elements with which to form judgments about the world. Their meeting had been affectionate, the tone was respectful, even devoted, and the occasion of that interview—his meeting with Nina in the bar in Talenti—had been mentioned just once, and not as the focus of an investigation, but as a convenient excuse for seeing one another again. Stasi returned home concerned primarily with the painful aftermath of his fall from the ladder, a persistent shooting pain in the middle of his back.

But he hadn't even entered the apartment when the phone rang. The voice of a young man, well educated, vaguely ironic, said: "Professor, did you find the page from Broch?"

"Pardon me, who is speaking?"

"A friend of Nina's."

"Oh, yes: I'm very sorry, but the book wasn't there."

Silence.

"My exam is tomorrow, I need that quotation. Go back and look more carefully."

"No, listen, I don't have time, what I was able to do I did."

Another silence. Then the young man said, with a sudden chill in his voice:

"They told me that you always do what you promise you're going to do. I'll be there in two hours. Make sure you have what you promised."

He hung up.

Stasi felt an old and obscure sensation that he had failed to hold up his end of the agreement. He looked at the clock, it was twenty past noon. Should he go back to Via Pavia? He thought back to the inspector, once again he felt the strong suspicion that the phone was being tapped. He felt his confidence in the effects of his professorial authority being rapidly undermined. He wondered why on earth his lessons would persuade Sellitto to become a guardian of the law and why the same lessons would convince Nina, on the other hand, to join an armed terror gang. He also wondered why both of them, from each of their differing viewpoints, would necessarily respect him and love him for the rest of their lives. He suddenly felt like an elderly professor who had overestimated the worth of the work he had done. Perhaps both of his former students, with their widely diverging choices, were evidence of nothing other than how little school really counted. Perhaps each of them, in a different way, was manifesting a fairly obvious impatience with and intolerance of him and of teachers in general: people out of step with the present day, relentless custodians of the distant past in its most sterile forms. Perhaps Nina was maneuvering him into performing an evil action, and Sellitto was poised to clap handcuffs on him, a dual movement of chance that had found its cruel point of leverage in the frailty of old age.

Suddenly he wondered: what if both of them were on opposing sides in a war, a subversive militant and a defender of the established order, which side would I take, who would I choose, for which of the two would I take responsibility, at the end of my life?

The answer came immediately. There was a long and winding thread, and Stasi seized one end of it instinctively, a conditioned reflex of his profoundly coherent worldview. For as long as he could remember, he had never wholeheartedly subscribed to the canonical forms of social life: the family into which he was born, the schools he attended, work, marriage, fatherhood. Stasi loved his own father, a lively, argumentative man, an employee of the state railroads from the age of eighteen—he was a conductor on passenger trains—and yet he rejected every word his father uttered, every thought that passed through his father's mind. He had strong ties with the family he grew up in, but he left home when he was young and turned his back on them. He was good at school, but he had always loathed every one of his teachers, he made a special effort to reject everything they offered him—he refused to adopt a single concept word, or manner of speech from his teachers. He married young, very young, and he stayed with his wife, Carla, till death separated them, but he always mocked the bonds of matrimony, and never wore a wedding ring. He had always been a doting father, spending lots of time with his daughters, but he spoke skeptically about fatherhood—he sometimes said that having children is an irresponsible act. Professor Stasi, in short, followed a secret path that now, at the age of sixty-seven, was very clear to him. He remained motionless, peacefully, like an insect on a wall. He was courteous even with people he disdained. He devoted attention to the less gifted and more troubled students, even when they were not easy to like; when a colleague fell ill, he was the first to pay him or her a visit, at home or in the hospital, whether that colleague was a friend or enemy; anyone who suffered—whether abandoned, defamed, or imprisoned—could count on his help, could confide in him, vent their frustrations. But he had always known that, if some greater force ever drove him to abandon his self image of a calm yet rigorous professor, a lucid but great-hearted thinker, then he would snap into action suddenly, like an apparently sleepy reptile darting its head violently from its lazy coils.

He put on his overcoat and hat again, walked out the door, and with his heart racing, he went back to the apartment in Via Pavia.

Corace's mailbox was overflowing once again, and this time, on the wooden countertop, there were also four packages of various formats and a couple of magazines. Stasi collected letters, packages, and magazines and went upstairs to the apartment. The rooms were so many bright patches of light, quite different in appearance from how they had looked by night, with artificial lighting giving them a yellowish cast, dotted with pools of shadow. The wooden blinds were pulled up, every polished surface shot reflected shafts of light. The professor minutely reexamined the bookshelves, picked up three or four volumes perched on a stool in the bathroom, rummaged through the books on the night table in the bedroom. The Broch wasn't there. Even though it was increasingly common for him to stare at things without really seeing them even when, as in this case, he was doggedly searching for something quite specific—it was as if a murky stream of water were flowing through his brain, washing away the "I am here, this isn't it, neither is this, here it is"—this time he felt positive that he had looked carefully through book after book, and that he had never wandered off in pursuit of a chance thought, word, or image. It was a pity, Nina's friend would be angry with him, Nina would stop remembering him as someone who always did what he had promised to do, and would start thinking of him as a senile old fool. But maybe it was better that way, after all. Aging is the slow process of becoming accustomed to the end of real life. One must slowly abandon one's image, one's role, and resign oneself to fading in the memories of others, and in our own. How long had it been since he stopped learning the names of novelists, essayists, directors, singers, artists, and notable people in general? When had he begun to cling to his customary books without trying to read new ones, to his old movie stars without curiosity about the rising ones? Five years ago, or three years ago? His daughter Ida would toss out a name of someone who, in her view, was famous, and he'd shake his head uneasily: he'd never heard of them. Becoming grey, melted wax, formless. Perhaps that was the best way to prepare to die. So many things die all around us. Ideas, interpretations, words, and phrases all melt in the warmth of the mouth, no matter how solid they originally appeared, destined to endure throughout eternity.

He took a closer look at the photographs on the wall, alongside the bed. There was one photograph of a group of people. There were nine young people, with beards, mustaches, long hair. Stasi perched his eyeglasses on his forehead and leaned in closer, peering. He recognized, with a degree of surprise, among the many faces that meant nothing to him, a colleague of his from three decades earlier, a colleague named Luciano, Comrade Luciano Zara. So Corace had known him too? Luciano had one arm around the shoulders of Nadia, a slender young bright-eyed woman with a page-boy hairstyle; Luciano had had a stormy affair with her that lasted a few months. Yes, it was them, there was no doubt about it. Afterwards, the affair had ended badly, she was a spoiled little bourgeois, she did her best to pretend to be a liberated woman, the way women were expected to be back then, but it didn't come naturally and she could never quite pull it off. One morning Luciano had asked Stasi to go to Nadia's house to pick up a suitcase containing his belongings. Stasi had agreed to do it out of friendship, as a favor, because one comrade should always be willing to help out another, without showing any proprietary interest in possessions, money, or time.

Who could say what those people were like nowadays? They had been the closest of friends, like brothers, for a few years, shoulder to shoulder they'd fought the same battle (a tough, fearless struggle), then they'd vanished. Luciano had even been a guest in Stasi's home for a few weeks, after breaking up with Nadia. Two or three days after Stasi had picked up his suitcase, Luciano had fallen ill, with a high fever, a hacking cough, and he had nowhere else to go. A bad case of bronchitis, teetering on the brink of pneumonia. He ate and slept on a cot in Stasi's living room. Each evening, the professor made him a bowl of broth, and his wife Carla fed him during the day, bringing him aspirin, fizzing and frothing in the drinking glass, and lozenges for his sore throat. Luciano did his part by entertaining the girls with wonderful stories; his boisterous laughter won them over, they laughed and laughed, unable to stop. Then he was gone. No one ever heard from him again, or from Nadia, or so many of the other comrades from those years. Stasi turned to leave, but on his way to the apartment door, he stopped to take a look at the mail.

So much paper. What did Corace do for a living? There was always a "Dr." before the surname. He received invitations to museum shows, conferences, lectures—there were eight invitations in this pile. There were also a couple of official letters from his bank. Stasi read through the table of contents of one of the magazines. He discovered, in a list of articles, all of them extremely interesting, a piece on the war in Iraq signed Carlo Corace and a sidebar on Iran with the initials "C.C." A university professor? A politician? A journalist? He set aside the letters and took a look at the packages. Three of them were made of corrugated cardboard, tightly bound by narrow strips of plastic; one was just a plain white envelope fastened with a metal clip and sealed with adhesive tape, clearly delivered by hand. He realized he was looking blankly at the back of the envelope, and turned it over to read the address. He saw with a genuine, childish burst of amazement that there was no address or postal markings. There was only a name, scrawled in script: Prof. Domenico Stasi.

His name. At this address. The package was for him.

He didn't even bother to peel off the scotch tape; he ripped the envelope open. Inside was the Broch, the old 1962 edition, it had a dirty white dust jacket with an ugly photo of the author. It looked as if it had never been cracked open. There was only one underlining, a phrase on page 46. It said: "Below, in the mists of the Underworld, the enslaved, domesticated masses toiled."

8

O nce he'd returned home, Stasi transcribed the quote on his computer, printed it, placed it in an envelope, and left it in the conciergerie downstairs, telling the concierge that a gentleman would come by to pick it up.

"What gentleman?"

"A gentleman, a young man, I believe."

"No, I mean, what's his name?"

"I don't know."

"I should give the envelope to whoever asks for it, Professor?"

"That's right."

The quote was almost certainly a signal, at least that's what Stasi thought. The young man would pick up the envelope and, depending on what phrase he found transcribed, he would make an urgent decision.

That struck him as the most likely explanation. Other hypotheses struck him as too fanciful. For instance, that the quote contained a secret message that could be deciphered by using a code or contained a specific word which, established and agreed upon in advance, indicated a decision. Or that the quote contained a formula that could be obtained, for instance, by taking the first syllable of each word ("Be-in-mi-o-the-Un-the-en-do-mas-toil"), and that formula was itself a message that contained an order: abandon a super-secret hideout or rob or kidnap or kill.

Stasi sat in his den and reread the phrase, this time with

aesthetic interest. He liked the expression "mists of the Underworld." Who knew what it sounded like in the original? The mists of the Underworld evoked the hypothetical canopy of the Overworld. And that's where I've lived my life, he thought, saddened. In this den, reading, learning. Learning what? The mists of the Underworld, studied and pitied from a comfortable chair, in safety, at the edge of the canopy of the Overworld, in a distant warmth. He had spent a life without great luxury, but without serious privations. I raised two daughters, and they live comfortably. I have rescued myself and my offspring from the harsh labor of pure subsistence, from ignorance, from the dust and the flies, the slimmest chances of survival, wars, from diseases without cure and without treatment, total lack of medical care. Perhaps the point is shame. I am unable to forgive myself for having taken my own flesh and blood to safety, while the blood of others was freely shed, rivers of blood, around the globe. I am ashamed that I did not remain with the domesticated toiling masses, the multitude of slaves below, even though, in reality, I myself had no freedom. Chained to a small salary. Careful not to violate the regulations of a state bureaucracy. A job that involved tedious repetition of things I knew all too well. No discoveries, no inventions. I never ventured too high, I never sank truly low, down where my own ancestors eked out a living until just one generation ago. I filled my mouth with a steady stream of words: I think, I say. Firm, clear, well informed words. The need for a revolution, everyone—everyone!—finally standing up together to take control of their own world. A constant struggle, where and however one is able. Die on your feet, rather than live on your knees. Rigor with oneself, competence in service to the helpless. I was the adult talking to children, until I grew old, in order to help them to grow up with the understanding that saving oneself—ourselves—alone is not enough, and that one's humanity depends on the degree to which we are sensitive to the down-trodden humanity of others. He heard the phone ring.

It rang.

Stasi answered, but with a slow gesture, a weary voice. It was Ida, with that resentful filial love in her voice.

"The doctor said Monday at ten."

"For what?"

"To show him the test results."

"There's nothing wrong with me."

"Are you a physician, Dad?"

Stasi said nothing, a melancholy half-smile appeared on his face. There were times when he suspected that his daughters' anxiety about his health concealed the hope that he might really develop a serious disease and die in the space of a few months, freeing them of the obligation to care for him.

"Okay."

"Okay what? Are you going to go?"

"If I said okay, that means I'm going."

He hung up. But the phone rang again. A raucous woman's voice said to him:

"Professor, we have received your order, thanks. We'll send you the merchandise on Monday of next week."

Stasi felt his heart grind to a halt. So the game wasn't over after all.

"What time?" he asked almost without thinking, as if he really had ordered something.

"At 10 A.M."

"Here at home?"

"Certainly, we'll send a messenger."

"At ten I have a doctor's appointment."

"All right, the messenger will be at your house at nine-fifteen."

"Thank you."

The woman didn't reply, "Thank *you*," but merely hung up the phone. Stasi stood up and walked over to the window. On the sidewalk across the street, he saw a fat woman, about fifty, with salt-and-pepper hair, sparse on the back of her neck, slipping a cell phone into her handbag. The woman looked up for a moment toward his windows, then she walked off, entered the park, and vanished among the trees.

Who were these friends of Nina? They phoned without any apparent fear that the line might be tapped. Thirty-five years ago, more or less—he remembered—it had been reported that the Italian intelligence services were illegally tapping at least two thousand phone lines. Nowadays tens of millions of Euros were spent every year on tapping phones. Illegality sanctioned by law triumphed, with a lavish squandering of public funds. This country is increasingly becoming a police state, he thought, anyone could be spied on. And so, what was the reason for their sloppiness? Nina's friends acted as if they were eager to be caught. Or as if everything in those phone calls— every phrase, every word, every syllable—were at once mysterious and perfectly innocent. Or, most important, normal. The envelope with the quote from Broch had been handed off to someone. In the passage from the book something had turned into a virtual command that he himself had imparted without intending to. The order had been carried out with satisfaction, perhaps even with gratitude. And he, for having picked up the book and transcribed the quotation, had perhaps earned a sort of gift pack, a final prize of some kind. Tea cups, a set of glasses, a blender. He went into the kitchen, he put some water on to make tea. In his tea he dipped a large handful of chocolate cookies, and listened to a radio program about politics and the economy, without really hearing a word.

9

Monday came, but slowly. Stasi arose early, readied the clear plastic sleeve containing his test results, and waited for the messenger to arrive. At nine fifteen on the dot, the entry phone crackled. The professor felt his heart crack open, opened the door to the staircase, and waited on the landing.

Coming up the stairs was not the typical young man in a motorcycle helmet with a chattering walkie-talkie strapped to his chest, but rather an older gentleman, perhaps the same age as the professor, with a distinguished air. He handed over a box wrapped in packing paper. That gesture of proffering was met with a corresponding gesture of welcome, of acceptance. No need to sign anything, thank you, good day. Yellowish packing paper. Color is matter, it renders opaque, it conceals. It contains. Stasi closed the door, set down the package with a sense of revulsion, alongside the folder containing his test results.

What was in the box? He sensed that starting up the game again would put him in a risky position, he felt a tremor in his hands, he wished he could talk to Carla about what he should do. He had lived happily with his wife, he had enjoyed their conversations. He was especially contented when he sat at his desk or in a chair, reading and archiving newspapers, magazines, and book until nighttime, and in the meantime he could hear her moving through the apartment: "Are you done yet?" "Did you brush your teeth?" "Why don't you come to bed?" He told her everything that passed through his mind, without explanations, as if even the thoughts he never put into words were still part of a conversation with her. And Carla would answer drily, with the ironic distance of a woman who had no foolish illusions. She'd tell him, you'll die like Pascal, my dear; Pascal worked right up until the end on the Paris road system. But it was clear that with the passing of the years, she had stopped thinking of him as a latter-day Pascal, and she no longer considered the things he studied as anything nearly as serious as the road network of a city like Paris. How he had loved that woman. He had discovered, with her, that if making love is often a sweet experience, making love with a person who appears indispensable to you in every aspect of life is the one pleasure in this world for which you never need to feel guilty. He had learned to be faithful to her without feeling his faithfulness as a burden, the forty-two years that he spent with her had been intensely fulfilling. When she had fallen ill, silence had gradually come to take her place. Now, without her footsteps, without her voice, and without her breathing, he could clearly perceive the creaking of the furniture in the apartment, the buzzing of the refrigerator, a slight humming sound that made him anxious. And now, in this new situation, a roll of the dice and his image as an elderly gentleman who had managed to grow old amidst a sort of general consensus ("You talk about subversive matters the way the saints often do," a priest and professor of religion with whom he enjoyed having discussions once said to him) would be defaced once and for all by an unsightly scrawl, bringing shame to his children and grandchildren, and even to the woman who had lived her whole life at his side.

Tear open, peer, touch, verify.

Or, perhaps, instead, put off, delay.

Procrastinate.

During the weekend, right up to Sunday, and for that entire night, Stasi had waited watchfully, overwhelmed with a sense of confusion. He'd read a little. He'd savored the old pleasure of words in the rooms of the silent apartment. He had realized that his life was a tepid observing of the world flowing by, along a ribbon of ink, he had realized that he wanted it to end in the same way. He asked himself, over and over, with a sense of anguished foreboding, why he had ever said yes to Nina. He no longer knew, perhaps he really never had known why. It was as if—he realized—his blood was running cold, as if his ardor had cooled. He sensed with increasing clarity that the ferocity of political and military behavior, the deplorable actions of the world around him and the world that extended out in the distance, the scandalous poverty of the many and the scandalous wealth of the few, no longer instilled that old sense of determination in him. The very idea that demons don't war against demons, that one Satan never exorcises another Satan, but that there are always hosts of devils on one side and hosts of angels arrayed against them, now struck him as a piece of rank sophistry. At the heart of the battle it is not always so clear where good lies and where evil lies. He realized that his words had become withered and jagged in his mind, that they slashed like shards of glass.

What did I discuss?—he asked himself now, on this Monday morning—what have I promised? It is true that I have believed, ever since I was a child, that time, this horrifying time filled with plunder, exploitation of man by his fellow man, extermination and genocide, this time that has gone on for at least seventy thousand years, had finally culminated. I sensed the impending arrival of the kingdom of God, or however I chose to describe it, here, and now, in the arc of my own lifetime, as though destiny had chosen me to be its little prophetic participant, in my work, in the rooms of my home, at my desk, in front of the television set. But prophecies are so many words. Nina instead—I now understand—is pushing me to act. And faced with a potentially horrifying action, the reasoning behind my indignation, even hatred, dries up, becomes arid. What sense is there to making the bad even worse? A ferocious guerrilla warfare. Open war. Civil war. Forced alliances that would soon explode into a bloody settling of accounts. And the secret requirements of History which, in the end, will justify as usual all the crimes and all the criminals, rewriting events, sweetening the pill, denying the facts. No, instead, just stay here, on the sofa, watching TV. I can't feel the lucid fury of someone who's decided that he can no longer take it.

Stasi left the package on the table with an impetus of horror, and instead picked up the clear folder and left the apartment. He arrived in the doctor's office right on time, but very uneasy and nervous. He sat in the waiting room, listening for his name, thinking about the box sitting on the kitchen table. What if a burglar broke into his apartment and, not finding anything else, took the box? Or else, what if Sellitto entered the apartment, like in the movies, to perform a warrantless search? The police frequently break the law. They knock down your door while you're sleeping, they beat you up, they torture you, sometimes they kill you; they are state-sponsored killers. Sellitto would find out what had been sent to him even before he did. He'd put two and two together, arrest Nina, him, the phone operators, and who knows what other people about whom he knew nothing. Or perhaps he'd do nothing, he'd just have Stasi watched, and let him continue doing whatever it was he was doing. He wouldn't stop Stasi until the considerations of high-level politics ordered him to intervene: make use of the senile old man, the cluster of idiots playing at terror conspiracy, exploit them as a way of criminalizing respectable citizens, young people, women, the elderly, people who fight everyday on behalf of genuine political needs. Even Corace would be arrested. They'd go over his apartment with a fine-tooth comb. They would examine the photographs, one by one, that he had on display behind glass, in his bedroom.

Every subject would be identified: friends, relatives. His address books, desk diaries, and electronic documents of every kind would be painstakingly investigated. There'd be cascades of arrests. Even the comrade Luciano Zara, present in those photographs together with Nadia, but now just an old man, though not quite as old as Stasi, would be investigated. That's how the police work: a daisy-chain, one name leading to another, toss everything into the pot, then wait and see. Thirty years after the fact, wherever he might live now, whatever work he might be doing, they would burst unannounced into Luciano's house, they'd pull open his drawers and rummage through them. Documents, old papers, you can always find something compromising. Who knows if his wife, Carla—Carla, who died suddenly just last year—ever wrote to Luciano.

I wanted to just leave that phrase lying there, artlessly, dangling without any immediate development. But it should burn into the eye of the careful reader.

(I rummage through my notes: "Nothing more than a glancing reference. Carla, Luciano. The opacity behind which Stasi sought safety." When I write a story—during the actual writing—I jot down ideas or characters that pop into my mind, even though the time hasn't come to use them: hypotheses about the nature of my characters, significant actions that this one or that one will perform either just a few lines down, or else further along, or perhaps at the end of the book, concepts that will serve to generate thoughts or dialogues. This material generally lies there unused, often I don't even look at it again, it's a memo that I almost never make use of. Recently, though, I decided to go through a number of stories that I sketched out over the years, including this story of Professor Stasi, for instance, and I pulled out the notebook with those notes. At first I planned to complete the stories that I still found interest-

ing and that I had left unfinished or incomplete. But then, suddenly, I changed my mind. It struck me that I could do something else: make use of my notes, my first drafts, and passages
that I had polished to provide a faithful, reliable account of the
drafting of each of the stories. A first draft is the closest thing
there is to life itself as it rains chaotically down upon our heads.
Why not give it a try? And so, here I am, now, trying to stitch
together what I had imagined for Carla and Luciano. For
Luciano, though, I have to remember to change his name.
Make a note, in case I actually publish this. I can't leave him
with the name of the colleague that I actually knew decades
ago, even though a real name is particularly comfortable for a
writer, while it's just depressing to give false names to a friend,
an acquaintance, a neighbor: Lucio or Luc or Z. or even
Comrade ***. The impression of authenticity, of truth, begins
to fade. Luciano was like this or like that, he used to do this or
that; now who is this Lucio, who is Luc, who is Z., who is
Comrade ***? Useless filters in a word that is so permanently
fake that it no longer requires filters.)

So the question remains: was Stasi's wife writing to Luciano?
If so, what did she write him? From what secret region did that
correspondence arise, assuming, that is, that there was a correspondence? Need to work on it. I have always had a certain fas-
cination with the topic of adultery, since my childhood, when I
heard my father shouting in the night, attacking my mother out
of jealousy, and I didn't understand, I didn't know whether
there was a reason for his jealousy, whether my mother really
intended to betray him, whether she already had, or whether he
was tormenting her, unjustly accusing her of it. Draw on the
episodes in which I suspected that I had been betrayed: by the
first girl I ever loved, for instance, when I was sixteen. Or else
draw on those occasions when, almost without noticing, distractedly, and then in an increasingly intentional, conscious
manner, I myself seduced someone else's woman, indifferent to

the ties of friendship, a stable marriage, trust, young children; and she, gradually, forgetful in her turn of friendship, a stable marriage, trust, young children, allowed herself to launch looks, complacent awkwardness and embarrassment, blushes, an open-lipped languor, signals of an incipient consent. And so, yes, tell the story of how two strangers begin to share the same sense of transport.

It's true; you never know when it happens, thought the Professor. A hand senses the distant warmth of another hand. Not the skin, but the clothing itself senses the grazing contact with the clothing of the person to whom we are attracted, as if the cloth were living flesh, densely riddled with microscopic sensory organs, a second skin. Stasi shivered with humiliation. He realized that the folder containing his test results was damp, that his hands were sweating. He looked around at the other patients waiting their turn. Many of them were elderly, poorly dressed, their faces unhappy, their eyes glimpsing images in their mind, not the reality of the waiting room, not the other patients. The professor was like them, alert and at the same time wandering, out for a half-hearted stroll, grieving, through little occurrences that he had long ago eliminated from his memory. It had been a mistake to offer hospitality to the Comrade Luciano when, after his break-up with Nadia, he had shown up, feverish, a solitary man, with no one to take care of him, at the front door of his apartment. In those days, though, there was no other way to behave. If a comrade was in trouble, you had to help him without thinking twice. You could never raise objections, for any reason, otherwise your regrettable nature as a member of the bourgeoisie would unfailingly rise to the surface or, even worse, petty bourgeoisie, the most detestable, a nature that manifested itself as a love of decorum, the folly of personal ownership, the cult of a tranquil routine, sexual repression, and grimy, narrow-minded jealousy.

Stasi knew that he was a member of the petty bourgeoisie. No, even worse, he was a southern Italian member of the petty bourgeoisie, but he did his best to behave in a way that kept this basic nature under control. If Luciano borrowed money, he never asked for it back. If Luciano took underage girls to bed, Stasi never objected, indeed he listened to the stories of these escapades with amusement, did his best to shield Luciano from scandal, from the investigations of the ministry of education, from the law, from the furious parents. Those were times of great enthusiasm and nothing, absolutely nothing, had a limit. If a limit did present itself, then the thing to do was cross it and go to see if people on the other side had greater freedom. To dare to say "that's not done" was a symptom of a blinkered mindset, it meant not only denying oneself happiness but, even worse, denying happiness to others. Stasi always did his best to keep from denying anybody anything. He believed that the only boundary that it was completely unacceptable to cross was the one that separated the forces of repression from the forces of revolution. Crossing that line was a mark of infamy.

Often the professor would tell his wife stories about Luciano. Carla always found it amusing to hear his accounts of that cheerful recklessness, and she generally felt an impulse of fondness for men who had successions of love affairs, lots of women, stormy relationships. Or perhaps it would be more accurate to say that she was critical of them, she scorned them, often she'd exclaim: he's a real shit! and yet she found them extremely interesting. For instance, she followed with great alacrity, through the stories her husband recounted to her, the whole story of Luciano with Nadia. She rooted for the girl, even though she didn't know her: her reckless abandonment of a marriage, her attempt to hold on to Luciano and the pain and suffering that went with it, along with a sequence of spectacular scenes and reconciliations; but Luciano's gluttonous overindulgence—she had only laid eyes on him once or twice in all—his joyful, and therefore fundamentally blameless frenzies, the way he rapidly tired of all his women, even when he seemed to be in the throes of a great and unrestrainable passion, put her in a good mood.

When Luciano came to live with them, he truly was in a pitiable condition, with a deep and cavernous cough and a raging fever. Carla welcomed him in with a slightly aloof manner, courteous but restrained. The two little girls, on the other hand, were intensely curious about this new arrival. They were young then, Ida was eight years old, Mena was six. They'd often creep up to spy on the big red-faced man tucked into his bed, a cot in the living room, breathing laboriously, coughing, hacking, and spitting. They tiptoed over to him and watched him, entranced, as he slept. But Luciano would suddenly open his eyes, imitating the voice of the big bad wolf just to make them laugh with the thrill of fear, and then he would send them off on numerous useless errands that they performed gleefully, running to get a marble as if it were a witch's eye, a puppet that was her evil assistant, a tiny teacup with a magic potion inside.

Stasi soon realized to his annoyance that he had lost the attention of his daughters; he'd come home from school and they no longer ran to greet him. Now they were interested only in Luciano, as if Luciano himself were a game, a sick dolly that they were going to doctor and nurse back to health.

Even Carla, to tell the truth, who usually greeted with delight every piece of nonsense that issued from her husband's lips, started laughing more and more often, and with ever greater amusement, at the stories and anecdotes that Luciano recounted. Though still suffering from a high fever, and constantly sopping with an unhealthy sheen of sweat—the living room reeked with a bitter scent—Luciano conversed playfully and laughed in his infectious manner. Stasi thought: that's the way he is, there's nothing I can do about it; there are people that have an aura; their bodies are built for success, they attract every human being that comes into contact with them, they exude a strength that gives strength to others; I'm not like that even in the eyes of my own family. In the evening, when Stasi brought Luciano a bowl of broth that Carla had made for him, and he sat on the side of the cot and helped him to eat it, even he felt a vague sense of pleasure, as if that gesture of assisting the invalid was, finally, the foundation of a cleaner, happier world.

Gradually, Luciano got better. He got out of bed, but he was still weak. He pretended that he needed the support of the girls to hobble from one room to another. Without them, he said, he would never be able even to get up from his cot, and they were proud to have been able to help him. It took him a long time to recover, his convalescence was longer than the sickness, but still neither Carla, nor Mena, nor Ida seemed to be in any hurry to send their guest away.

In the evenings, when Stasi came home from work, he sensed a crescendo of excitement, as if his daughters and wife had forgotten what the passage of time signified, and they were vigilantly monitoring the passing minutes, savoring their novelty and delight. Once, Luciano even sat down to play Carla's old piano—as a girl she had played, not very well and not very ambitiously—and the girls had run to watch and listen. He started out with *Frére Jacques* and then launched into a series of increasingly fanciful variations until Carla came into the room, listening in open-mouthed astonishment, and he finally stopped abruptly, saying: let's go play a game. Another time Mena and Ida both burst into tears simultaneously at the idea that Luciano might recover from his illness and leave. And on yet another occasion, the girls kissed him goodnight, and then told him to kiss their mother goodnight too, and there was a burst of embarrassed laughter from Carla, who gave Luciano a loud smack on one cheek; he returned the kiss, but sliding down until his lips found her earlobe, her neck. Stasi felt defenseless, vulnerable. He felt that Luciano needed to vanish from their lives. He took him aside, a few days later, and told him with courtly benevolence: it's starting to get a little crowded here, you're better now, it's time for you to find another place to live.

Luciano left immediately with calorous thank-yous all around, he said how grateful he was for their help, and that was the last they saw of him: Stasi and he exchanged the occasional "ciao!" at school, and that ended quickly as well. Soon in fact, very soon, he vanished, moved to a different part of the city, or left town entirely, perhaps went into a different line of work. Secretly, without a word to anyone, awkwardly, bitterly, with feelings of insignificance and inadequacy, Stasi even wondered if Luciano might have joined one of the violent militant groups of the late Seventies, and had gone underground. He had suspected, from the time he'd gone to pick up the suitcases, that Luciano was capable of it.

Mena and Ida soon forgot him. Carla never asked about him. Instead, she became very jumpy, tried to calm her nerves, decided to use her savings to buy more fashionable clothing, a table for the living room, a new television set, and a sofa on which to sit more comfortably in the evening, when they watched whatever the television had to offer. She was suddenly dissatisfied with everything in those years, she said increasingly often that life, the things she did, everything seemed devoid of meaning. It occurred to Stasi that maybe Carla and Luciano talked on the phone, met, wrote one another secret letters, with countless cunning stratagems. He puzzled over it for a while, then his wife seemed to regain her tranquility. All that seemed to linger was a certain disenchantment in everything that she said, even in her expressions of love, even in her care for the girls.

"She's different now, I've lost her," the professor thought to himself occasionally, with the unhappy detachment of those who know that the worst is over but what remains is no longer what used to be. How painful it is to know that something has changed even though it is still there, right before our eyes, apparently exactly as it was. She was identical, and yet Stasi knew that every gesture, every glance had a secret weave to it that he could not detect. I wanted to focus on the nuances of those thoughts, and their effects. I wanted to succeed in conveying, subtly, that the professor felt, as it were, as if his own body had suffered a demotion. Stasi should understand, suddenly, now, in the doctor's waiting room, that in the long-ago instant when he had sensed that there was an intense emotional bond, a bond that extended over distance and separation, linking his wife and Comrade Luciano, at the very moment that he had realized this bond was also throttling something that belonged to him, he had also perceived, three decades earlier, in 1976, a sort of ethical earthquake devastating the little world to which he was still clinging.

Everything, the generous hospitality, the loyalty, the mutual assistance, the crystalline rigor, the solidarity, the sincere trust— it had all been revealed to be a fraud, a façade. He felt stupid, and moreover there was a trace of enchanted religiosity that now prompted only a cold fury in him. The candor of the saint who attributes his own candor to everyone else. Comrade Luciano was not a subversive battling for the redemption of humanity. What redemption? He had, through no merit of his own, a certain aura. It was a predatory aura and, like all auras, it stole, from those who possessed the least, the few things that they owned. He did it without even meaning to, beyond the things he said, beyond the articles of faith to which he subscribed, even beyond his possible heroic role as the leader of a column of an armed militant group. It just happened, that was all.

"Stasi," the receptionist called out.

Stasi leapt to his feet, as if the doctor might get tired of waiting and leave if he took a second too long. He detested his obedient haste: he slowed his steps, moved at a more leisurely pace. He entered a dark hallway. The door was open. He walked in.

"May I, Doctor?"

"Please, make yourself comfortable."

He sat down across from the doctor, a doctor with a furrowed brow.

"Your daughter tells me that you are somewhat out of control."

"No, not at all, I just don't want to waste your time. The results all look routine to me."

He handed over the folder with the results, and the doctor pulled out the sheets of paper, running his expert eye over the test numbers.

"Good, very good," he exclaimed, as if good health were the fruit of diligence. Stasi smiled, he needed to feel that he was meritorious, he wanted to be encouraged to do well.

Then the doctor frowned, and he looked at one of the numbers closely. He stood up and walked around behind Stasi, who watched him in confusion, turning his head slowly, his neck bones creaking with pain as he did so.

"May I?"

"Please."

The doctor pressed two fingers under his Adam's apple, at the base of his neck. Stasi felt bewildered, as if he had lost all sense of forward and back, inside and out, up and down. He murmured:

"Is there something wrong?"

"Nothing. A slight problem with your thyroid, Professor."

Silence.

"What could happen to me?"

The doctor smiled at him with a reassuring expression and went back to sit at his desk.

"The worst that could develop is a goiter."

Stasi left the doctor's office with a new battery of tests to be done. He thought: I didn't tell him anything about falling off the ladder, the pain in my back. Now he felt a certain irritation under his Adam's apple, where the doctor had palpated it, and he was experiencing difficulty in swallowing. When his cell phone rang and Ida asked: "Well, Dad?" he answered nonchalantly: "Everything's fine. Just a minor thyroid problem."

His daughter's voice quavered with worry.

"Don't kid around."

"I'm not kidding. I'm fine, the doctor told me so. I just have to take a few more tests, but there's nothing wrong with me."

He had a hard time persuading her. She told him, as angry as if he had intentionally done something spiteful, that she was going to call the doctor, find out for herself, learn the truth. "Sure, that's fine, go ahead and call him," Stasi replied calmly. "I'm going to call him, Dad, that's right, you see if I don't call him." Go ahead, he thought to himself. The doctor would tell her about test results, the hospital, ferocious scalpels, organ extractions. The time remaining to your beloved father, my dear woman, is short and drawing shorter. Oh my god . . . That's right, ma'am. To heal is to torture. In either case, the body, I'm sorry to say, is sadistically wrenched. Living flesh twists and turns in agony and pain. Knowing it, foreseeing it gave Stasi a sense of euphoric giddiness. The impending punishment of the flesh, the only place that punishment could occur, made him desire a growing burden of guilt. He wanted to splurge into guilt, in order to win for himself, to truly deserve, the definitive loss of self.

He stopped at the public park.

The park was squalid, trash nestled in the lawns, here and there a condom. He sat on a ramshackle park bench. He was surprised that a word like guilt should have popped into his mind. The guilty—he had always believed—are those who exploit, plunder, starve, devastate, exterminate, and poison.

Those who simply react to crimes against humanity are guilt-less, even if they shed a great deal of blood. Blood does not stain the just man. It may provoke horror, but shedding that blood is in some cases necessary. He sighed. Now he perceived distant images, all dating back to the remote past. The long-ago ambition to achieve absolute innocence, for example. To suffer an offense and yet not react. To separate two who quarrel, never to be the third party who benefits from a dispute. To suffer evil, and never to commit evil actions. A sacred alliance with the weak. When he was a small boy, he liked to imagine himself as the Blessed Domenico Savio, who later was canonized as Saint Domenico Savio. He was well dressed, with a cravat, his face slightly wan and dull because of the goodness in his gaze. The faces of the just always have pale eyes that never flash or glitter. Stasi had committed himself, as a boy, to having a gaze like that. He aspired to have the generosity, loyalty, and courage required to place himself between the furious combatants who sink fangs into one another, beat one another, shatter each other's bone with a horrifying sound, and do evil to the peace-makers. He wanted to be devoted to the Virgin Mary and her son Jesus. He thought that this was meant to be his life.

Once, in the springtime, he actually felt a burning sensation on his ribs. He pulled up vest, shirt, and undershirt and found a red patch on his skin, ringed by a purple border that felt as if it had been seared. The patch transmogrified horribly over the course of a couple of hours. It spread, turned whitish in the middle, and was covered over with a granulous patina. After a few days—Stasi remembered with a horror that had never faded through the years—after a few days he discovered that within the purplish perimeter the surface of the patch was undulating. Hard, dense beads were springing up, one next to the other. When I ran my finger over the surface, they no longer felt like living flesh, but some inanimate material. I thought that my whole body would be covered with those pearly beads each one linked to the next. I was all alone with a spreading patch—perhaps it was malignant or perhaps, certainly, why not? it was a sign of the goodness inherent in my nature; I was developing wounds like the flesh of Christ. I didn't want to show the patch to my parents and ask for help, I was afraid to show it to any of my friends. I preferred to remain in a state of uncertainty, to think anxiously of the patch, sometimes as of a heroic yearning for suffering, at other times as a burning brand of guilt, something horrible that I had done without realizing it. I was afraid that if my mother had seen the shiny little beads, she'd cry out: Ohwhatahorriblethingwhymyson?whymyson? As for my father, he would have howled with disgust as if my diseased skin were his own. And so I decided to keep my suffering a secret, I lived in the lurking anguish that my mutation might be discovered, and a medical or religious authority might explain to me that this was the brand of evil. The definitive—and most greatly feared—sign that I could not become a saint like Domenico Savio, I didn't have the right stuff, no Don Bosco would knit me a blessed tunic. I was too vulnerable, too fragile, slimy. One week later I went to the beach with a group of other children: we had to take our clothes off to go into the water. I covered the mark of my mutation with one hand, to keep the others from seeing it on my ribs. I dove into the sea, and swam both on the surface and underwater. I got lots of sunlight, and at the end of the day I had a bad sunburn. The next day, the little beads began to subside, and they had soon turned into a hard, shell-like bruise that was almost indistinguishable from the sun-burnt skin. Before long, there was nothing left, the evil had been concealed, or else the goodness had been hidden for good. And so I stopped dreaming of sainthood. Often, by pure chance, people turn their backs on callings that are well within reach. A seraphic thought of goodness that was just starting to take root vanishes suddenly, along with the humble, priestly voice that you were just starting to acquire. And yet kindly thoughts, words of comfort, cordial mediation, and a tone of optimism are all agreeable things. For instance: why take it for granted that there is something terrible in the box on the kitchen table? Evil thoughts. Why not believe, instead, in a gift from Nina or from that Corace or even from the young man who needed the quotation from Broch for his thesis. A box of chocolates. Expensive tea, a teapot. Books. Stasi stood up from the bench and hurried home.

He opened the package.

In the box was a pistol and a photograph of a puffy-faced bald man—his face was hairless as a baby, with tiny heavy-lidded eyes, so squinty they seemed shut. No instructions: what he should do, where he should go with that weapon. Only the pistol and the photo.

The professor sat at the kitchen table, staring at the gun and the picture. He reached up to touch his throat, where he could still feel the impression of the doctor's fingerprints. He discovered in that moment the truth behind the expression: "I am speechless." He was mute, even inside his brain. I have emotions, feelings, but I can't sense them flowing through my nervous system. It's happened, and what's happened is right here. Bewilderment. Fear, but as if viewed from above and to one side, as if he were muttering: There, that's what fear is.

10

I worked for days on Stasi's fear, drawing on what I had experienced when I thought that the man I'd tangled with on the bus had come boldly to stand outside my house, planning some unthinkable vendetta.

He's watching me, I had written in my notes, swept away on a wave of anxiety. But the man didn't look like someone watching another person, he looked like someone waiting. Moreover, he was definitely younger than the person I had attacked, he might have been thirty years old. I realized this not only by scrutinizing the photographs, which I had later downloaded into my computer, but—let us say—also by studying him directly, many days or a couple of weeks later, when I saw him at the covered market, with a woman.

The guy was at the fruit stall, and I was at the fish stand. He was built physically like the other, older guy, that much was true: he was big-boned, he had a large head, and they both had a gangling gait. But the resemblance ended there. He certainly lived in the neighborhood, his companion must have been his wife or his girlfriend, and she was big herself, with an imposing mass of curly black locks. I quickly forgot about both of them. It was not until I had paid and was about to leave that I glanced over at them, and it struck me that the woman was looking at me and, caught in the act, she immediately shifted her eyes away in embarrassment.

Exaggerations, really, But they helped me to move the story along a bit. I thought quite a bit, for instance, about the infi-

nitely changeable reactions of bodies. One minute you feel as if
nothing could hold you back, the next minute your intended
victim suddenly frightens you. The instant before, it seems
absolutely reasonable for you to think about killing a man, and
the next instant you're disgusted with yourself, you feel weak,
incapable of acting. On the bus, when that bully insulted the fat
black woman, I lost all sense of proportion, the respect that I
thought I had felt all my life, first and foremost the respect for
other human beings. Not only: I had drawn the words with
which I expressed my murderous rage from the deepest layers
of my mother tongue, not the standardized Italian of the Fifties
and Sixties, which were the years in which I was educated—
and my Italian dated from that period—but Neapolitan, the
Neapolitan of the Forties, the language of my childhood:
stuchiavechemmèrd, *stufigliecàntaro*, *stustùppolo*, *stucèsso*,
obscenities and insults that evoked bloodshot, bulging, rage-
engorged eyeballs. And then, slowly, I had calmed down, The
sweat had chilled under my armpits, it seemed to me that I was
emanating an offensive body odor. What holds us together in a
community? Nothing.

A community is held together with spit. A community is the
memory of something that once contained us and which we
don't want to admit we have left behind us for good. It is distant laws. Abuses. Thickets of lawyers, magistrates, policemen.
An encrustation of the fear of chaos and death. There are
bonds of affection, occasional ties of solidarity, but they count
for nothing. In contrast, hatred—now there is something that
endures, is powerful, and cuts like a steel wire. The lust for
blood, its pulsing purplish flash. Theoretically, you can sup on
it whenever you like. Hatred and desire lie just under the frosting of good manners, of good morning, be my guest, pardon
me, take your time, and thank you. All it takes for a neighborhood soccer team to want to cut the throat of the barista across
the street is her sarcastic show of rooting, with a sneer, for the

rival neighborhood team. All it takes is the tenant upstairs who insists on hanging her sheets out to dry, depriving our bedroom of light. All it takes is a racket or a din, music playing too loud after midnight. Just a careless shove in the street. Someone staring a second too long at your woman. A community always knows, deep down, that its members have nothing in common, it's all just unfair competition, market forces, divergence, fracture, illegality dressed up to look perfectly legal, a violent preservation of the balance of power, prison, terror artfully scattered by the government, concentration camps (or stadiums: the horrible Chilean stadium to which the thugs and torturers of the US and Pinochet confined the opposition; all that rebellious fury I savored and gave voice to, that's what that stadium really was, proof positive that Fascism is the remedy when the masses fail to vote as they should).

Time went by. Now the story was languishing, especially the plot. I was dangling Stasi motionless, in front of the pistol and the photograph, overwhelmed with emotions, and I couldn't bring myself to make him do anything. I had sketched out nine short chapters, and I'd revised a few of them, while others were laid out with actual memories of mine that needed to be disguised, or complex notes on the actions Stasi was to take. I was stopped cold before the usual blank space, a milky body of water, formless and empty, and I didn't know whether I'd be able to ford it. From time to time, I'd fiddle around with screenfuls of prose and, depending on my mood, I'd add phrases, cut them out, or isolate them.

Then I went to the Turin book fair, in May, I think, to present to the public the new book from Fandango, the one that was being published to provide disaster aid, a red-and-blue book entitled *Openings*. We talked about it in some hall, I can't remember which, maybe the yellow hall: we were well dressed, well fed, rosy-cheeked, and safe. Alessandro Baricco said that he felt it had cost him quite a lot to print the first chapter of his next book in advance; it wasn't the sort of thing he was used to doing, but he'd been glad to do it, to help out the survivors of the tsunami. I spontaneously said, well, all things considered, it wasn't such a terrible sacrifice. And he replied, drily: what would have been a sufficient sacrifice, in your view? Breaking a kneecap?

He was right. I tend to exaggerate. I'm not truly good-hearted, I'm not truly generous in spirit. I think of generosity and goodness as extreme manifestations, and the small good deeds performed in situations of comfort, the little acts of generosity, the ones that don't cost you an arm, a leg, an eye, three fingers, or even your life, strike me as small potatoes. I needed to give Professor Stasi—this went through my head while the other writers were speaking—an abstract tension toward doing good. I should have him reflect, for instance, on the passage in the Gospel of Mark in which the wealthy man, in great earnestness, falls to his knees before Jesus and calls him Good Master. Jesus responds: "Why callest thou me good? there is none good but one, that is, God." I could have Stasi say, in desolation: No, no, goodness, there is no goodness, not even Christ is good, and he is the son of God, goodness is not incarnate in the flesh, a good schoolmaster is only an obedient employee in the service of the wealthy man reluctant to give away all his possessions, if you really want to be someone who teaches, you have to venture toward the cross, a real professor never teaches according to the good and reassuring beliefs of the conventional conformists. Therefore, I need to push the professor, step by step, to remember when he was a little child, when he discovered in his heart not a good nature, but something else, more burdensome, the ferocious and desperate demand that he be absolutely good. And develop the reference to Domenico Savio, for instance, dredge up out of memory the huge impression that the child-saint had made upon me when I was small.

I jotted it down in my notebook, after the panel discussion about *Openings*: Domenico Savio, find out the year in which he was beatified, and the year he was canonized, and if necessary, make Stasi a few years younger or older. I remembered him holding a lily, in prayer, but I could be wrong. He was held up as a model to the children of good Catholic families during the Fascist era, but on into the postwar years as well. Teachers were supposed to try to emulate Don Bosco, dedicated to preventive education, and scholars were supposed to be like Domenico Savio, students of holiness. Stasi, at the peak of his anxiety, had something like a relapse into childish religiosity which, bubbling up from beneath his atheistic belief system and secular moral convictions, suddenly poured forth out of channels that he had long forbidden himself, revealing the source of his exaggerated sense of goodness. Behold, then, Saint Domenico. Have him take part in the action. Maybe even give him wings. I liked the expression "taken under the protective wing." Write a history of that metaphor. The protective wings of Egyptian, Assyrian, Babylonian, Hebrew, and Christian cultures.

I liked that idea, I was almost tempted to mention it in public, but the opportunity never presented itself. I exchanged a few words with noted Italian author Sandro Veronesi, who was another one of the writers who had made a contribution to the benefit book. The beginning of his novel struck me as extremely well-done. About mine, he said that it seemed to point in a direction that reminded him of *Atlantic City*.

Atlantic City? I remembered little or nothing about *Atlantic City*, I felt stupid. My *Atlantic City* opening chapters?

I looked everywhere for a copy of that movie so I could watch it again, but I couldn't find it while I was in Turin, and I still haven't found it. I went to a bookstore, though, and looked in a copy of the Morandini film dictionary. It said that *Atlantic City* was directed by Louis Malle, and it tells the story of an elderly gangster and a young woman who asks him for protection:

he agrees and kills the people that are trying to hurt her. That's the plot. I don't know if the film really has anything in common with *Claim for Damages*. I hope not. In fact, I doubt it. I would say: absolutely not. Certainly, in my story too there is an old man and a young woman. But good Lord, if we pay attention to this kind of comparison, you wind up back with Susannah and the Elders. The story is heading in a different direction. I am writing, it strikes me, about how old age reconciles mental habits formed of extreme reactions. Perhaps I need to look for other film plots to find resemblances, the history of literature and film is a catalogue of all possible stories. But *Atlantic City*, I don't think so, no, I'd rule that out.

On the trip from Turin back to Rome, I tried to calm myself. But the fact is that writers need confidence, at least I always need it a great deal. I returned home with great misgivings. I set the story aside, even more perplexed. It was a good thing that I had decided to make public only those two chapters. Sandro V. had been honest and straightforward, I should be grateful to him, perhaps he was only trying to encourage me. The days passed. Then, little by little, my story, after its humiliation, began to revive, and soon filled my head: again, and more than before. How should I carry on with it? I'd make Stasi the same age as me, that was safer. I have to redo the encounter with a doctor, I had already written a similar encounter in *Ability and Liability*. The two daughters, Ida and Mena: I wanted to write that after much back and forth, Mena, the more rigorous of the two, demanded a very strict distribution of days. On even days, she'd be responsible for their father, on odd days it was her sister's turn. I meant to sketch her out as a pleasant, cordial woman who, however, inevitably, with kindness in her eyes, always winds up speaking ill of the people about whom she started off, with great determination, saying good things—including her father. Ida, on the other hand, I want to portray as angry and prickly: every word she says carries a sting, she blames her father for having taken away her mother's joy of life, but still she manifests a genuine apprehension for the old man, as if she were capable of reading in him the symptoms of his decline and feeling—not affection, no, but a little pity. The rest, for now, can be left to its own devices. In the dribs and drabs of spare time, I do Internet research, I am focusing on Domenico Savio. This is stuff—I said to myself—as far as can be imagined from Burt Lancaster, Louis Malle's crepuscular gangster. Let's just try to imagine that Burt Lancaster had a childhood obsession with Saint Domenico Savio; unthinkable!

11

S tasi sat motionless as a marionette, facing the package he had just opened. Domenico Savio appeared behind him, in the kitchen, a miniaturized version of the saint. He fluttered his smallish wings, wings like those of a kestrel. He landed on the nape of the professor's neck, wrapped his faded wings around him protectively, covering his grey hair, his fleshy asymmetrical ears, one larger than the other. The very tip of the saint's feathers stretched down to the base of his neck, grazed his diseased thyroid.

So what did the saint do in his brief life?

He was born in 1842, he died in 1857. An existence that lasted fifteen years, three of them beneath the pedagogic heel of Don Bosco. Domenico Savio was declared a hero of Christian virtue by Pius XI, ten years before I was born, in the heart of the twenty-year Fascist regime. He was beatified by Pius XII in 1950, when I was seven years old. He was canonized by the same pope in 1954, when I was eleven. Today you can purchase online a special maternity apron, an *abitino*, that he himself tied around the neck of his mother, pregnant for the eleventh time, experiencing serious problems with the delivery of the child.

"I remember him with an appearance of cleanliness, neatly dressed, neatly groomed," I have Stasi think. There was always an aura of light around his head. Oh, to be like him. No more dirty ears, dirty feet, stained clothing, no more hair that refuses to stay in place even if you glue it down with soap. I needed to abandon the tantrums, the fistfights in the courtyard, the scabs on my knees. I planned to go to confession more often. I planned to become a close friend of both Jesus and His mother. I resolved to stop exercising my wee-wee by trying to thrust it into a hole that I had carved into the wall, in a secluded corner of the house. I wanted to be a saint too. Domenico Savio had my own first name, the priest had told me that *Domenico* meant devoted to the Lord, it seemed to me that I had an inside track, and my mother was a seamstress just as his had been (but his father was a blacksmith, while mine was a railway conductor). That was a time that I think back on with pleasure. Nothing seemed able to hurt me anymore. I never cried myself to sleep with tears of rage. If someone insulted me, I no longer responded with a string of obscenities, I no longer ran to the schoolteacher to tattle. If two boys got into a fistfight, instead of standing around like all the others, watching and yelling *scommal'e sangh* (Neapolitan dialect for reducing someone to a bloody pulp), I would rush between them, doing my best to separate them, proudly taking kicks and punches without hitting back. I secretly hoped for an outbreak of cholera in Naples—there was a very reasonable likelihood of such a thing—so that I could go courageously to help the sick. I said Hail Marys constantly, I've never said so many in life.

During those years I was especially fond of the Madonna. She was young, beautiful, and had a quality all her own, a specific virtue that in catechism was referred to as the Immaculate Conception. The light that surrounded her was deeply moving. I never appreciated light the way I did in that period. I hoped that light would gather in a nimbus around my head the way it did for the Virgin Mary and for Domenico Savio. To love the Madonna. To have the sun shine upon you even at night. Or in any case to be endowed with a particular yellowish electric energy that made you stand out, that distinguished you, that clearly said: this, ladies and gentlemen, is not just your ordinary melancholy boy, with a railway-ticket taker for a father, who howls with displeasure, a seamstress mother who weeps in humiliation, lots of snot-nosed little brothers and sisters, never a penny to spare at home, a child that is sad—ever so sad— because of the unhappiness of those he loves. This child is illuminated night and day. The light was like that of the star of Bethlehem, bright against the dark blue of the night sky. A luminous wake. Or even the tail of a dazzling bright dove. I aspired to have a body baptized with the Holy Spirit, a warm gust of devotion, a breath that had a luminosity that was every bit as good as anybody else's. I wanted to be aflame with good intentions and loving impulses.

Then, suddenly, a liquid wet my underpants. The desire for sainthood was swept away. To be truly good, like Domenico Savio for example, began to seem impossible to me. At the very utmost it was possible, with a great effort, to be good some of the time, and this drained me of all energy, to be partly good struck me as repellent. I wanted to be a saint or else to masturbate until I bled. As wretched as I felt, as foul and filthy, I began to perceive my own name as a burden, the name that had previously sat as light as a feather. Now I was studying Latin. "Devoted to the Lord," suddenly seemed to me, to my disgust, etymologically, an expression that spoke of servitude, subordination to a master. My father added his own two bits of information: he told me that I was by no means named after Saint Domenico Savio, but after Saint Dominic de Guzmán ("San Domenico" in Italian), a hard-hearted inquisitor, a torturer of free-thinkers. That settles it—Stasi remembered thinking as a boy—I have a veritable vocation for evil even in my first name. And so he decided to abandon the idea of sainthood. For the rest of his life, all that remained to him was an aching nostalgia. And now this sudden fantasy of having the saint clutching his head and neck. He brushed him away from the nape of his neck with one hand, the way you might with a pigeon fluttering overhead, the little saint was holding too tightly to his throat with his wings, his claws. Domenico flew away after putting up some slight resistance, and rapidly perched on the pistol and the photograph. For an instant, the professor he had the fleeting impression that with his tiny hands the saint was lifting the pistol and pointing it at him. He smiled in resignation. Then even he, Saint Domenico Savio, was willing to do evil in order to prevent evil. As always. The saint was willing to shoot him between the eyes—isn't that how they put it in detective novels, in thrillers? or should that be: he was willing to bust a cap into his forehead?—if he wound up deciding that he would comply with the wishes of Nina's friends, above all if he felt closer to them than to Sellitto, the law, the state, the banks, NATO, and the elite circle warming itself in the light of the Overworld.

12.

I thought back to the direction the story had taken at the beginning, before I had begun to write, but as I thought about it before falling asleep, and it struck me as an octopus with many tentacles.

There was Nina, who had been arrested. There were her parents. There was the phone call from the elderly professor, the meeting at the café in Talenti, a request to go pick up a package. I hadn't yet thought of the apartment on Via Pavia, there was no Broch. The professor, without any further complications, goes to pick up the package from the cashier in a box office of a movie house on the outskirts of town. Once he gets home, however, his curiosity gets the better of him, and he cannot resist taking a peek. Inside he discovers a pistol. In the meantime, he receives further instructions, this time by mail. He is told to go to Genoa, hand over the package to a young man who would be waiting for him at the station bar. The professor is tormented by doubt, hesitates, and finally decides to go.

Thus begins an anguished, excruciating train trip. Suspicions, disquieting faces, obscure phrases. The Intercity express rackets north apathetically, from time to time the sea appears, blue flakes pasted to the windows. For hours Stasi (who did not yet have a name, at this point) sits in a second-class compartment with five noisy young people—aged about twenty-five or thirty, southern Italians—who laugh, joke, and argue. There are three men and two women, and they are talking about a job interview scheduled for the following day, they all have university degrees, one young woman has two. At a certain point, they stage a contest to see who among them has more credentials and a longer resume. The professor focuses, however, on the language they use. They could have been former students of his, he thinks. But they don't talk at all the way he did when he was growing up and studying, there is none of the effort he had made ever since he was a child to flee his dialect as if it were a curse, to construct a magical eloquence, useful for extended discourse. His language had been structured for use in an affable mediation: it seized, contained, restrained. In contrast, the five young people have a broken, throttled way of speaking. If he had been asked to transcribe it, Stasi would have had to use numerous ellipses and dashes and question marks, even inside individual words (one of the young people often used the word malignant, and it sounded as if the word were being torn apart vowel by vowel in his mouth).

It isn't that they speak badly, it's that their speech is broken. The closer the train comes to Genoa, the more the professor realizes that something toxic, a poison, is issuing from the fissures in the phrases. The young people recount to one another their despair over lives that have passed thus far without compensation, for the hard work they have pointlessly lavished on their studies. They believe that they are well prepared—all-too-well prepared—to sail triumphantly through the world that awaits them, and so they hate the obscure enemies that are preventing them from doing so. They detest the old people who refuse to retire into old age, they detest the people their own age who use family connections to obtain important positions effortlessly, undermining the rules of fair competition. They detest the managers, the masters, the internships. They detest politicians, the prime minister, the leader of the chamber of deputies, the president of the senate, the president of the republic, all the institutions and, especially, at that moment, the state railways and the ticket taker who passes through, asking "tickets, please, tickets, please." They detest Stasi, sitting silently in his corner: the foolish old man, and perhaps they even murmur one to another, snickering: old *'nzallanuto*, Neapolitan for a madman or, to be precise, one driven insane by the goddess Selene. One of them, a young man with red hair and a broad white forehead, often employed, with a feigned enthusiasm, the verb "to merchandise": hurray, he said, the global institutions of merchandising have even merchandised the air we breathe.

Stasi—in this version of the story—tries to comment just once:

"The bosses are looking for obedient personnel. Education makes workers disobedient."

The young man with the pale white forehead shoots back immediately, irritated at the intrusion:

"Disobedient? All they need to do is tell me what they want, and I'll obey. I want a boss, I'm dying to have a boss. The problem is that nobody wants to order me around."

At the station of Genova Principe, the professor gets out of the train hastily, his old body and mind intoxicated by the rage and hatred that his young traveling companions have emanated throughout the compartment. When he is approached in the station bar by a young man, about thirty, with a mustache, Stasi hands over the package containing the pistol and asks, anxious to please: "Is that what you need, is there anything else I can do?" The young man says nothing other than "No, thanks," and walks listlessly away, passing close by the noisy little group of young people his age from the train.

The professor then eats a *panino*, and catches a train back to Rome. This time, he is seated across from a bottle blonde in her early fifties who soon turns out to be disgruntled teacher. They speak of this and that, they admire the view, the gardens, the colors. The woman occasionally savors with courteous irony the sound of words such as acanthus, privet hedge, boxwood.

Stasi says, with the same delicate and courteous irony, that he adores the light of the lemon trees. Cue curtain.

I went on like this for weeks. The faces, the landscapes, the voices, the links between one episode and the other were like waking dreams. The elderly professor's face resembled a teacher I had had in high school. I saw his hat, his overcoat, I heard his voice, he was a well-defined, independent person. Real images (a ticket taker or the station sign—Genova P. Principe—or the station bar the way I'd seen it at four in the afternoon the week before) set off mental sequences and I lived in a state of distraction for a period that felt endless, but might last only a moment, a fleeting instant. Everything seemed to press in upon me with a vigorous coherence. But as soon as I attempted to marshal everything into written form, the story seemed to lack realism, sociological detail, a fundamental narrative syntax in a way that depressed me.

Then one day I set to work writing and the train, the station of Genova Principe, the well educated, unemployed young people all vanished. In their place appeared Ida and Mena, Sellitto, Luciano Zara, unexpected developments. And now I had arrived at this point, here, with Stasi motionless, staring at the box he had just opened, at his fantasy of a minuscule Saint Domenico Savio, the hallucinatory image that was rising gradually, from the seabed of his adolescence, like a clear bright bubble, to the murky surface of old age. The saint wanted to prevent the professor, by force if need be, from transforming the sunset of his life into an evening of evil. Or perhaps not, Stasi thought, perhaps he is encouraging me to act out of love for the poor and the oppressed. He's not aiming that pistol at me, he's trying to hand it to me, he wants me to do as an old man what I failed to do when I was young.

I read it, I reread it.

How to proceed from here.

I felt a deceptive tug, a jerk that, while it was dragging me off into a political thriller with guns, ambushes, and blood was paradoxically preventing me from finding the tense dramatic pace that I wanted to impose on the story, and it twisted it into sarcasm.

It occurred to me that I might describe the unexpected arrival of Ida in the company of Stasi's other daughter, Mena. The two women—three years' difference in age, both of them about forty—show up by surprise with their children, the professor's young grandchildren: Ida has two daughters, Mena has a son (or the other way around?). They ring the doorbell once and then Ida, without waiting, opens the door with the key that she keeps in case of emergencies. The professor manages to conceal the pistol just in the nick of time, but he leaves the photograph on the table. Ida and Mena burst in to the apartment. They treat their father with agitated concern, they are worried about his health. The little girls immediately try to capture their grandfather's attention, first one then the other, tugging at him alternately. The boy, seven years old, perhaps eight, waits for the grandfather to decide on his own to pay attention to him, and sits, to one side, in disgruntled silence.

"Grampa, did you know that my tooth fell out while I was eating and I swallowed it?"

"Really?"

"I have a new bracelet, do you want to see it?"

"Yes."

"But the tooth fairy put a coin under my pillow anyway."

"There's no such thing as a tooth fairy, stupid. Grampa, you want to try on my bracelet?"

"Doesn't the tooth fairy exist, Grampa?"

"Yes."

"You want to try it on?"

"Yes."

"You see? He said the tooth fairy exists"

"She doesn't exist. Grampa told you that so he wouldn't hurt your feelings, right Grampa?"

"She does too exist. Isn't that right, Grampa, she does exist?"

Mena, who had a degree in chemistry and worked in a small manufacturing concern in Valle del Sacco, was less nervous than Ida, and therefore more observant. It was she who, at a certain point, noticed the photograph on the table and said: "I know who this is, he was in the newspaper today, I don't remember his name but he's an officer at ENI, the oil company, tomorrow he's going to be in Rome to meet with the prime minister."

Stasi was astonished. A highly placed ENI executive: what newspaper was it in? Then he lied: "I found the photograph in my mailbox, it's some kind of advertisement."

In the meanwhile, the silent little grandson, Michele, turned the photograph over and over in his hands, looking at the back, and in order to get a little attention, he read aloud, as if it were a classroom exercise, but with the grumpy pride of a male displaying his skills in order to teach his enterprising little girl cousins a lesson: *Execution, 26 March, 11 o'clock, Hotel Hassler, Room 317, cancel.*

Soon, however, I changed my mind. I liked the encounter with his daughters, it struck me all as fairly natural. Ida kisses her father on one cheek with a loud smack, Mena withdraws, evading his arms, ironically objecting: "No, I'm not kissing you, you reek of flounder." There is a lengthy stretch of dialogue, variously affectionate and resentful, continuously interrupted by jealous interjections from the young nieces. At the end, Ida's daughters steal the photograph from their cousin, they're playing with it, they call out: "Look how ugly he is, he looks like you." But I came to the conclusion that the family atmosphere did nothing to elevate the tension of the story. As for the boy's chance discovery of the writing on the back of the photograph, it struck me as a tiresome contrivance, and so I discarded it.

Instead, I started to imagine that, just as Domenico Savio was picking up the pistol with his tiny hands, the intercom buzzed from downstairs.

A burst of anxiety.

"Who is it?"

"Sellitto, Professor, is this an inconvenient time?"

"Why, no, come on up."

Stasi barely manages to get the pistol and photograph back into the box in time. Now he's flustered, as he opens the door and admits his former student. Sellitto enters, he's affectionate, almost like a son. He speaks with a slight sense of apprehension, skillfully guiding his words along the line between the spoken and the unspoken. "Take care, professor, Antonia Villa is not as innocent as she might seem. This Italy is murky, there is detritus deep down. You think you're playing your own game, but you're really doing the bidding of hidden powers. The puppeteer is often a puppet himself, you know, I remember you taught a whole lesson on this point, it made an impression on me. I am paid by the state," continued Sellitto, "to watch the show, evaluate it scene by scene, and shut down the production only if shutting it down serves a secret script, a carefully devised superscript that was crafted, what do I know, at the Italian Ministry of the Interior, or the Foreign Ministry or in Washington or maybe in the caves where Bin Laden is hiding, or where his carcass is rotting, you name it."

And so on.

In my mind, the whole time, from one topic to the next, the inspector grazed, touched, and shifted the box that sat on the table, a few inches this way, a few inches that way. Finally, as he was about to leave, he said:

"Let's say, hypothetically, that there is a packet of particularly compromising material in this box, and that I know about it.

Well, do you seriously think that I would come here and arrest you? Not at all. I have to decide whether arresting you is more useful than not arresting you, I don't know if I make my point."

"It's perfectly clear."

"So you see how complicated my job can be?"

"I see."

"You are too restrained, Professor. Is that what happens when you get old? Like one of those characters in American movies who never loses their cool, no matter how complicated the situation becomes?"

"Why would I need to lose my cool, Sellitto?"

"I wouldn't know. What I do know is that, whatever your age, you have to fill up your life with something, otherwise you feel like a living corpse. I know a director, Professor, he's about to make a movie. If you want to do some acting, I could give him a call and ask him to find a small role for you."

"I'm not an actor."

"I know that, but I've read that when people get old, secret drives and impulses come to the surface, unachieved fantasies, repressed talents."

"That's not true of me."

"Certainly not. But one of my colleagues, a woman, her father has been married twice, four children, who knows how many lovers in his lifetime, well, they caught him the day before yesterday giving some Senegalese a blowjob in a movie theater near Termini Station."

"You think that's likely to happen to me, Sellitto?"

"Of course not, I'm just talking here. But, if you need some help restraining yourself—you know what I mean, a person is suddenly seized with a yearning, a yen, he wants an ice cream, and there's a gelato shop right across the street, so he makes a beeline in front of oncoming traffic, practically with his eyes shut, he doesn't look both ways, all he sees is the gelato shop on the opposite sidewalk—if you feel that kind of a yen, why don't you give me a call? Here's my card, that's my phone number, I'll come running to hold you back. Those streets you cross with your eyes closed, Professor—they can be dangerous."

Sellitto knows something, the professor is thinking at this point. Yes, the inspector seems to know more than he does about what's happening to him. He has come to his apartment to tell him, in that allusive, perhaps grievous way of his: take care, you're getting yourself into trouble, I'm here to help you, trust me. The minute his former student leaves, Stasi reopens the box with none of the calm that he's made such a show of until now, he overturns its contents onto the table, polystyrene beads bounce in all directions. Only then does he discover written on the bottom of the box, in pencil: *Execution, 26 March, 11 o'clock, Hotel Hassler, Room 317, cancel.*

This was the beginning of a slow movement, I needed to orchestrate it carefully.

And so this was an execution. But an execution at whose orders? At the orders of subversive forces guided by a foreign state? On behalf of a god that loves one state but hates others? In obedience to our own Italian state, with its long and venerable tradition of secret crimes? An execution on behalf of the humiliated and the abused who have never had a state or any power of their own? The professor was repelled by the word "execution," it summoned up the idea of a cold taking of life, a pistol shot to the back of the neck, blood; and yet he felt no urge to chase Sellitto down the stairs, show him the message and the pistol, entrust himself to him. Quite the contrary. He diligently erased every word, blew away the scraps of eraser, and in the meanwhile imagined the crimes of the man he had been ordered to shoot.

There was no point in beating around the bush. That man was to be the latest victim of the new Red Brigades. Nina—the inspector had hinted to him elliptically—was a member of the new Red Brigades, a young woman at war inside a country that pretended to be at peace. The man in the photograph had been sentenced to death in some clandestine council meeting. Perhaps he was just a low-level clerk. Perhaps he played an important but shadowy role, a secret adviser. Perhaps he thought of himself as just another professional, someone doing their job. But almost certainly—this seemed indubitable to Stasi—that person, even if he himself was unaware of it, blinded as he was by the values of present-day society—was acting or had acted on behalf of those who crush millions of lives underfoot in the Underworld, who poison bodies and the entire planet, who deny aid to the victims of some new, latter-day plague, who help to drive stock prices sky-high by manufacturing weapons, selling them, unleashing wars, and massacring innocent victims.

The professor stared for a long time, with a growing sense of curiosity, at the tiny, slit eyes of the man who was sentenced to die. He was familiar to him, a brother, like Cain. Or like Abel. The fury of blood shed out of greed. The fury of blood shed out of a need for redemption. He knew that these were two twin madnesses. He knew that neither one ever amounted to anything good. And yet, he checked the state of the weapon with old, nearly forgotten gestures of hand and eye that dated back forty-five years, from his military service. It was loaded.

Still, even this version didn't work, didn't flow properly. It was important, admittedly, to have Sellitto resurface in the story, but maybe I was having him say too much, or too little, maybe this wasn't quite the right time and place to bring him back on stage. And then there was the problem of the message: on the back of the photograph, on the bottom of the box. Didn't it smack of novels from bygone days? Wouldn't it be better to have the instructions delivered in a text message on Stasi's cell phone, or in an e-mail with the photograph as an attachment?

I thought of using Domenico Savio again. No daughters, no grandchildren, no Sellitto. Only the professor and the ghost of that saint from his early adolescence.

Stasi—here's what happens—Stasi shoves the box away from him, polystyrene beads scatter across the kitchen floor. He stands up, he walks slowly toward his office, but Domenico Savio, who has grown in the blink of an eye to full human size—now he is a young man, aged about thirty, a fine broad pale forehead, taller than the professor, rail thin, eyes glistening deliriously—says to him in a tone of admonishment: "What about the pistol, what about the photograph?"

"I don't know what to do with them."

"I can explain, if you like."

"What do you think you can explain? You don't know anything about this sort of thing."

"I know when enough is enough. You are too accommodating."

"If you're not accommodating, sooner or later there's going to be bloodshed."

"Does anything ever really change without bloodshed?"

"No, nothing does. My life has passed by, so many things have happened, but substantially nothing has changed. Capitalism continues to be just as ferocious, the exploitation is harsher than ever, democracy is increasingly just a procedure of assuring that the rich remain rich with the electoral consensus of the poor."

"All the same, you're too accommodating."

"What else can a person do? I hope that charitable acts, solidarity with those less fortunate, and good sentiments can save us."

"How? By handing out a few crumbs to the victims of gross depredations, with the magnanimous approval of the predators?"

"There was a time when you believed differently, you separated those who quarreled, you tried to bring peace."

"A waste of time. Those who quarrel find a way to get back into the mix, and the strongest one always wins. There's no way to take power peacefully from the few who hold it and hand it over to those who have never had it. There is no good magic that can perform that trick, there's no intervention of blessed or saint, there's nothing."

"I've known that for more than fifty years."

"So?"

"When I was young, I thought that violence was a curtain to be drawn with a necessary gesture, unemotionally, as a way of letting in a little light. Now it terrifies me."

"Why?"

"I don't like the fable of the emperor's new clothes anymore, yet I am afraid of seeing things as they are, naked."

"Maybe you're becoming an old hypocrite."

"I don't know."

Stasi speaks quietly. He recounts, in little more than a whisper, the fear he had as a boy: that he might fail to recognize the horror, or that he might tolerate it, exactly like the previous generation had done. He had wanted to live with his eyes wide open. But he had noticed far too many horrifying things far too late, and other horrible things, at the time, he had considered acceptable. Now he has an increasingly difficult time saying with any certainty: I am on the side of justice and right. The urban guerrilla warfare that takes up arms to strike at the heart of the state seems to him, despite the justification that it enjoys, a form of murder that strikes out at harmless individuals from ambush, identical in reality to a Mafia or camorra gunman. The suicide bomber who has suffered all manner of abuse and who therefore, in the name of his god, destroys both himself and other lives no less unfortunate than his own, struck him as a peculiar shadow on the walls of a planet on the verge of some final disaster. Both urban guerrillas and suicide bombers, moreover, in cases where they did not strike with violence, but instead wrote documents to explain what they aspired to achieve with the political, religious, and military actions, demonstrated clearly that they—precisely like many politicians ensconced firmly in the public institutions—were the product of the exceedingly mediocre mass education that he himself had helped to perpetuate over the past fifty years: crude minds ready to set up gulags and execute by firing squad, and torture.

The young saint looked at him compassionately: "Are you saying that you don't have the mind you once did, that old age is changing you?"

Stasi shook his head no, and sat down in front of his computer and turned it on.

"Change me how? The ideas that today seem new are older than the ideas with which I've looked at the world for decades. I rejected them half a century ago, why accept them now? They want to make you believe that rich people are suffering unfairly and need help, that poor people are having too good a time of it and need to make some sacrifices. These aren't ideas, they're con games."

"So?"

"Maybe we were wrong. Maybe the human race never had any hope at all, and struggling to redeem it is like lighting a purifying fire that only destroys the object it's intended to purify."

"You know that this is a senile rant?"

"Yes."

"And do you know what a senile rant is in the final analysis?"

"What?"

"This is a deviation toward another Stasi who no longer has words of confidence, a skeptical, half-asleep Stasi, who reluctantly accepts what little there is that's acceptable in the world and, out of love for his daughters and his grandchildren, holds tight to it out of fear that things might get worse. What do you have in mind? Are you planning to become a proper name and nothing more, without any determination of your own?"

"No."

"Are you sure?"

"Absolutely. But how can I manage not to feel fear? The rebellions going on around the world are risky: they either have muddled objectives or they are trying to establish bloodthirsty theocracies."

"Everything that undermines the regime of the bosses is risky. But just because you're afraid of running a risk, does that mean you want to help *your* mortal enemies to fight *their* mortal enemies?"

Stasi made a vigorous gesture of refusal, and muttered phrases under his breath, the way old people tend to do once they are engaged in the pursuit of their inner visions, alone but convinced they are in the company of the past. What he feared more than anything else was losing, as the phrase goes, face, becoming an empty organism, a phantom. And so he quietly rejected the wave that was dragging away his beliefs, grabbed back the words of his identity, and smiled with a hint of melancholy. I'm nearly seventy years old, he murmured, my back aches, my thyroid is in bad shape, my stomach can barely digest anything anymore, and yet it's as if I was about to take passage on a ship as a cabin boy. This is what living too long can condemn us to. The excessive duration of bodies and brains becomes a wild card, an internal contradiction of the system. Old people try to keep alive ideas and tensions from fifty years ago, and with a vigor and energy induced by prescription drugs, they make surprising lunges in this direction or that, untimely, prompted by a youthful urge to act.

"What should I do?" he asked feebly.

The saint laughed.

"Check your e-mail."

Stasi obediently clicked on the mail icon.

As usual, there were messages of all kinds: group e-mails from teachers' associations, announcements of cultural initiatives, Trojan horses designed to unleash viruses, humanitarian petitions to be signed from every corner of the globe, international advertising for Viagra, obscene proposals, and finally a message from an odd e-mail address: lintarsiatore@yahoo.it. He opened it with a sharp stab of his index finger. He read: *Execution, 26 March, 11 o'clock, Hotel Hassler, Room 317, cancel.*

Stasi deleted.

Okay, enough, too much talking. I decided to put off to the second draft the decision on the best, fastest, most economical way of having the professor discover the task that he had been assigned to perform. For now, it was enough to say that he had a pistol, a photograph, and a deadline. He could decide either to go to the Hotel Hassler or not. In the fourteenth and fifteenth chapters—the most difficult ones, I knew I'd have to work on them for weeks—I would need to tell a difficult story: how a person acts without making a decision, how they marvel at everything themselves first and foremost. I was planning to make use of two episodes, one from my adolescence and one from when I was a young man; I had already jotted down some notes about them.

I turned off my computer, I noticed that there was a beautiful afternoon light. I went to the living room to chat with my wife for a while. The few times that she is in the house (she's usually at work all day), I have the impression that I write better, more freely, as if her footsteps in the other rooms were a sort of metaphysical sentinel that keeps an eye on things to ensure that the words work out successfully.

But the phone rang. A woman's voice—a heavy, uneducated voice—asked if she could see me right away, even for just ten minutes, it was urgent. I wasn't that surprised. It happens fairly often that I receive phone calls or e-mails or text messages with this kind of request, and they always seem to be urgent. Sometimes they are female readers, less frequently male readers, quite often former students in some unhappy period of their lives. I replied only:

"Do I know you?"

"No."

"What's your name?"

"It would mean nothing to you."

"Tell me anyway."

"Mina."

"Like the famous singer?"

"Like my grandmother."

"Mina, I'm very sorry, but I'm very busy right now."

"I only asked for ten minutes of your time."

"I'm writing something right now. In a few weeks, though, I expect to be finished with the first draft; could you call me back then, and we can have a coffee together, okay?"

The woman murmured in a pained tone of voice: "My father can't wait that long."

"Your father?"

"My father is the man you attacked on the 495 bus, remember?"

She said that she was outside my apartment building, she'd take no more than ten minutes of my time. She added, with a subtle sarcasm: "Then you can go back to your writing."

I was alarmed: "How did you get my address and phone number?"

"With a little patience."

I told my wife that I was going to step out for a breath of fresh air; I didn't want her to be alarmed. I crossed the street, and I met Mina at the café directly across the street from my apartment building. She was sitting at a table in a corner near the plate glass window, and she nodded to me as if we were old friends. I recognized her; she was the heavyset woman with the dark curly hair, that I had seen at the covered market. I sat down, ill at ease and reluctant, and I ordered a cup of coffee. I said in an openly unfriendly tone of voice:

"I only have enough time to drink an espresso."

"That's all we need."

She began by saying that she was actually doing me a favor. She had called me to take care of a matter that, if neglected, might easily turn ugly.

"I don't understand what you mean."

"Do you remember my father?"

"Not particularly. He had insulted a woman, and I stepped in, that's all that happened. If someone were to insult you here right now, I'd do the same thing again."

"No, professor, that's the way you remember it, that's the way you tell it, but that's not the way things really went. You attacked him, you insulted him, you physically assaulted him, you threatened to kill him, and you terrorized him."

She told me, in an increasingly agitated manner, that her father had come home in a state of prostration. She said that they had had to call a doctor. She said that the doctor had sent him to the emergency room at the Gemelli Polyclinic, and that he had immediately been admitted as a patient. He said that all the doctors were astonished: he had been a healthy, robust man until two hours before, and now it was as if something had broken inside him, as if something had snapped. They had examined him and done numerous tests to determine what had happened.

"And what's wrong with him?"

"He has a fatal disease."

"Oh."

"A malignant tumor."

"And what does all this have to do with me?"

She took a moment, perhaps consciously. She took a slow gulp of her Coca-Cola.

"It was you that caused it."

I stared at her in astonishment. I told her that was absurd, strong words don't cause tumors. Her father must have been sick for a long time without knowing it. These diseases, I pronounced in a pedantic tone of voice, are insidious. That's how my mother died: she had a case of hepatitis, nobody noticed, it led to cirrhosis. The disease lurks for a long time, in some cases, before exhibiting itself: we are highly hospitable organisms. I held up both hands in a desolate gesture. A young waitress dressed in jeans and a checkered shirt brought me my espresso. "I'm very sorry about your father," I said, "but a disease runs its own course." Her father had experienced a misfortune, she needed to resign herself to that fact.

She shook her head, as if I'd never spoken, and reiterated: "My father had only one misfortune, and that was meeting you."

"Look, he'd be sick even if he'd met the Pope."

"Don't make fun of someone who believes in God and who has a particular need of their faith in this unhappy moment."

"You're right, please forgive me."

She nodded ever so slightly, and compressed her lips to convey the idea that she was doing everything within her power to keep from crying.

"You see, my husband and I are simple people, we know that life is a matter of good intentions. But my brother is different from us, he's just like my father. You can't imagine what we've gone through, trying to calm him down."

I drank the rest of my coffee.

"Please send your brother to see me. I'll talk to him. In fact, tell me if I can go visit your father, I'd be happy to go see him."

The woman shook her head.

"The best way for you to resolve this matter is to talk to me."

The verb angered me, and it alarmed me as well.

"What do you mean by 'resolve this matter'?"

"We're looking at some major expenses."

I sensed that I was about to lose my temper.

"You're looking for money?"

"When someone does serious harm to someone else, he needs to pay for what he's done. It seems to me that's the only civil way for all of us to put our minds at peace."

I gave her a chilly smile. I stood up, took a ten Euro note from my wallet, and laid it on the table.

"I understand. My dear lady, the only thing I can do for you is to pay for your drink."

This time, Mina looked at me uncertainly.

"Maybe I didn't make myself clear."

"Oh, you've been perfectly clear."

"You don't know what my brother is like."

"And I don't want to know. Good day."

I turned my back on her and in great agitation I left the café. It was she who had no idea of what the fury building up inside me was like. Let her send her brother to see me, right then and there. I asked nothing other than that.

13

I concealed the pistol and the photograph in one of the pockets of the bathrobe that I kept beside my shower stall. It struck me as a safe place: who would ever go rummage in the pocket of a faded green bathrobe?

I had a hard-boiled egg, a bowl of salad, and two apples for dinner. The apartment was too silent for me. I turned on the television. For a solid hour I watched a show on TV, then I took half a tranquilizer just as I have done every evening since Carla died, and I went to bed.

Unlike on most nights, the tranquilizer didn't cause me to sink into a deep sleep. Instead, it only liberated a sequence of images of uncertain texture and substance. At times they seemed like daydreamy memories, at other times it seemed as if everything was happening in the present, but not in my bedroom: instead, it was in the kitchen in my parents' house.

I was fifteen years old, it was Christmas Eve. My grandmother was sitting quietly in a corner, her eyes were bright and lively but she was immobile, curved like a pruning hook. She was a tiny creature nearing the end of her existence, her grey hair gathered in a bun on the nape of her neck, her mouth twisted sharply to one side as a result of a stroke. I felt sorry for her, now she could only express herself with her eyes. By rolling her pupils, she was indicating a package on the counter by the sink, wrapped in heavy yellow paper. She was inviting me to do something, fondly requesting a favor, or perhaps it was a command issued by an elderly woman with an unquestioned authority all her own. Evidently my mother, my father, and my siblings were all somewhere else. I was alone in the house with her. She wanted me to take her place, and perform a task that she could no longer carry out because of her damaged body. I obeyed: I never said no. I felt like a stone rolling down a steep slope, dragged irresistibly downward by its own weight. I knew what she wanted me to do. In previous years, ever since I was a small child, I had been a horrified but attentive spectator, I had memorized my grandmother's every gesture. I went to the grey stone sink and I put the stopper in the drain. I picked the package up from the counter, I could feel it writhe and thrash. I emptied its contents into the sink; a welter of female eels—the ones that in Italian we call *capitone* because of their outsized heads—flopped onto the stone surface.

My grandmother seemed to approve. Then I took a large knife out of a drawer; until only recently she would never have allowed me to touch that knife. It had a broad blade, and its edge had recently been honed on the grindstone. I pretended to be relaxed, and made all my actions reflect that charade. I went back to the sink. The eels were beginning to untangle, they were slithering their bodies softly one against another. I can't say how many of them there were. I remember a living dark substance, with occasional silvery glints.

I seized one with my left hand, it slithered away with sinuous motion leaving a slimy encrustation on my palm and fingers that I found disgusting. I wiped my hand on my trousers and, at the same time, I used the tip of the knife to shepherd back into the sink one of the eels trying to make its escape. I felt a mixture of disgust and frustration, I wanted to win my grandmother's approval, but so far I had failed. I turned to look at her and my gaze met her lively mobile eyes. I turned back to the eels, I seized another one, but this one too slithered out of my grasp. I tried again and again, I stopped bothering to try to wipe off my hand. One eel would slip out of my hand, and I'd quickly grab another. I soon realized that though it was true that their bodies were slimy cylinders that were very difficult to hold on to, still, my body felt a fundamental horror at touching them, it pretended to obey the command to seize the eels but it wasn't really willing to grip them firmly, it would grab them and then give up. At that point, with an angry gesture, I pressed one down with my palm flat, just below the head, on the bottom of the sink basin, as if I wanted to punish not the eel, but myself, for failing to do as duty required. Then I wrapped my fingers around it, pulled its full wriggling length up into the air, and whipped its greenish living body furiously down onto the counter surface, a violent slashing blow, and then tried to pin it against the stone so that I could carve into its flesh with the knife blade. I have to cut its head off, I thought, while my heart pounded painfully in my chest, and I plunged the knife downward. From that moment on it felt as if the blade were a part of me, I could already sense the animal's resistance from the black veil of its outer skin. I sawed the blade back and forth, the flesh opened out revealing its fat, squishy, whitish interior, I cut deeper, cracking the bony part, and I could hear my respiration, deep and noisy. I could also feel my teeth gritting and grinding, I saw the fish thrashing and gasping. I thought to myself that it had a mouth with teeth just like mine, its eye seemed like a peephole into the eel's life, signaling: I am about to end. The knife finally slid down to grind against the stone, and the eel's head separated from its body.

I did it again, and again. I carved the eel to pieces, as the segment with the head continued to twist and strain, its mouth agape, the eyes pieces of living flesh that remained alive despite the mayhem, the faint trail of blood and slime on the stone like a path of drool from the sliced flesh that continued, stubbornly, to attempt an escape. Each piece refused to die, it arched, thrashed, and blindly sought to reunite its nerve ends to the those belonging to the rest of its body. I continued to cut doggedly, ferociously. I sliced away with a furious repulsion.

Then I realized that the sink was empty. I turned to look at my grandmother; her eyes were rolling in alarm. I wondered how long she had been trying to attract my attention, trying to tell me that the other eels had escaped. I laughed nervously with the knife in my hands, I squatted down to peer along the floor, under the furniture, beneath the sink. I pretended to find it funny, but there is no joy when eels are fleeing in all directions in a kitchen at Christmas time. There's only the frenzy of the hunt. A living creature escapes, another living creature pursues it, that's the way matters work. I am a chimpanzee following slimy tracks. Deal out death, receive death. I was trembling in my bed, I felt as if my whole body was aching.

Now maybe I really was asleep. My grandmother was talking, my grandmother who hadn't been able to say a word for months. She told me that eels live on worms, that they eat snails, peas, and beans, and when they want to, they wriggle up water pipes, they climb up them in search of a way out, they come out of the faucets, out of the sinks, they slither all through the house, and they climb into your bed while you sleep. I dreamt of the invasion of the eels and I was aware that I was dreaming. My grandmother was immobile in her chair, a paralyzed monkey, a bonobo that could no longer play, her eyes alive with terror, and long, fat, big-headed, female eels slithering under her skirt, reappearing between her remarkably buxom breasts. I awoke with a start; it was four in the morning.

I made coffee. Today, I thought, I'm going to call Nina's parents. I took a shower; in the mirror I saw a ravaged body, I hastily concealed it beneath my bathrobe. For the first time, I found the faded terry cloth objectionable; Carla had selected it years ago, the same color for her and for me. The pistol was still in the pocket, along with the photograph. I dried my hair, I smeared a cream over the wrinkled, cracked skin on my face. At nine on the dot I dialed. Nina's father answered, and he made no secret of his annoyance.

"Nina's gone back to her own apartment."

"Can't you give me her phone number?"

"I can tell her that you called."

"Please, Signore Villa, it's absolutely necessary that I speak to her."

He gave me her home number, he said that he couldn't remember her cell phone number. I called her immediately, but the telephone rang uselessly for a long time. I draped my bathrobe over the radiator, I got dressed, and I went outside. For once, I didn't buy the day's newspapers. I strolled for a while, doing my best to notice the park, with the white of the daisies, the pleasure of the warm early-spring breeze. I was astonished by the tiniest and most nonsensical things: grass growing between grooves in the stone, light glittering in a basin full of water by a drinking fountain, young women running to catch a bus, a small round Filipina who stood carefully applying makeup to an older woman seated on a low wall, children shouting with happiness as they rode down a shiny slide, even the liver spots on my hand. I noticed a young black man sitting on two piles of old books, his back against a closed metal shop shutter, with a shoe on one foot, his other foot bare, as he carefully polished the other shoe. Walking through a muck-covered underpass, I almost tripped over a boy who was about to shoot up a syringeful of heroin; the needle—I actually only really noticed the needle—looked to me as if it were made out of a precious metal. I walked through dirty parts of town and clean parts of town, I noticed sheltered children and street urchins. Rome is dazzling, on certain days, and the light magnifies the filth and the danger. Everything seemed as if it were set carefully in the right place, in just the right way. If someone were to die in the street right now, the death and the blood and the disgust at the broken body lying awkwardly on the asphalt would simply turn into a lovely interplay of bright colors. I went back home, dialed Nina's phone number again, though without any hope. This time, however, on the other end of the line, someone picked up the receiver.

"Nina?"

Silence.

"Nina, I'm sorry, I urgently need to see you."

"So?"

I laughed, awkwardly.

"I did what I could, Nina, but I can't do any more."

"So?"

I added: "At least, I don't think I can."

"So?"

The line went dead.

A sense of moral failing once again swept over me, as if on some occasion I had failed to behave with the nobility that I attributed to myself, and now I was at a disadvantage. Nina was barking at me by phone, proving to me that she remembered perfectly well the reaction she had had in class when she was sixteen. You're a cowardly dog, she was saying, you bark but you can't bite. Sink your fangs into flesh. Right great wrongs with other wrongs. Those who wield power, it is well known, are always in the right. To rebel, rise up, rip to pieces not at random, but according to the orders given by a strategic command, with bold adherence, and not just in the realm of ideas. But I had already pulled back during the Seventies. I was revolted by the kneecappings, the kidnappings, the political assassinations: a stupid disgrace. I imagined the shattered bones, the lacerated vital organs, and I experienced a sense of vertigo that made my stomach lurch into my throat. All the same, a secret part of me—even when the unfortunate human being that had only recently been alive but now weltered in a pool of its own blood could not possibly be anything but a harmless victim—was unable to avoid feeling affinity with the killers rather than with the killed, with the kidnappers rather than the kidnapped. I deleted words of condemnation from my vocabulary, I tried not to use current labels. I was careful, even in my thoughts, to avoid using the words murderers, criminals, torturers, terrorists; I felt that they were somehow inadequate. I really thought of them as combatants. Of course, their actions filled me with horror, even fear, and yet the stand they were taking, the determination with which they were attacking, wounding, taking prisoners, and taking life as if they were metaphysical surgeons doing battle with a tumor, led me to feel somehow, I'm not sure how to put it, indebted to them, almost as if I owed them something for having acted in my place, sparing me, at least for the moment, tensions, anxiety, and disgust. That "so?" from Nina, that sign of the impossibility of any reconciliation, both frightened me and fascinated me. What a beautiful day, I thought. So? So? So?

I stepped out onto the balcony, I checked the health of Carla's plants, and I groaned at the pain in my back. Her plants had new leaves, fresh buds, they were in excellent health. I had taken very good care of them, I had not lost one since my wife had died. The plants were alive, she no longer was. Everything passes, life goes on by virtue of a horrifying oxymoron: it endures by dying.

I thought of another scene of death. My grandmother's time had come to an end, by now. The custom of slaughtering animals in the home was disappearing, the merciful skills of those who knew how to take life and then make dinner were vanishing. Women no longer killed chickens in the kitchen, they no longer dunked them in boiling water and plucked their feathers the way my grandmother had done for years. But once—I was just a little older than twenty, Carla and I had been married only a short while—the father of one of my students brought me a live hen as a gift.

Carla was still a young girl with ponytails fastened with rubber bands, a beautiful smile, and a slender body. She looked at the hen.

"What do we do with it?"

"We eat it."

"Alive?"

"Dead, of course."

"And who's going to kill it?"

I've said it before, I always try to do what I think other people expect of me. My wife left the kitchen, she went to shut herself in the bedroom. I examined the chicken which was lying on the floor, next to the sink, its legs bound together. Its plumage was white, the comb was pale, and its eyes looked panicky. I realized that I could no longer remember how my grandmother slaughtered chickens. With a club? With a knife? With a sort of karate chop, a single sharp blow? I rummaged around for a knife, but the era of well sharpened knife blades was also coming to an end. The only knives we had in the kitchen were ordinary table knives. I lifted the animal up, laid it on the marble counter next to the sink. I put its head close to the basin. I thought to myself that it must have a carotid artery, a blood vessel that, when opened, would simply pump out gushes of blood until the hen died of blood loss. I felt beneath the neck feathers. I could feel my cold fingers plunge into a vaguely damp warmth, I felt the cool air on my fingertips when I pulled my fingers away again. I gripped the knife, held the throat firm, and cut down.

Nothing happened, it was the wrong kind of knife. I tried, using all my strength. The feathers were spattered with blood, the hen pecked at thin air, gurgled, protested, and turned a flaming red eye on me. A thin stream of dark blood began to trickle into the sink. I opened the faucet with the right hand that gripped the knife, the water began to run, mingling with the blood. I was holding the hen in place with my left hand, its heat was surging up my arm to my shoulder, my chest, and my heart. I suddenly found I was covered with sweat, I could feel that my shirt was damp and cold on my back. This is what it is like to take a life, I though. Beneath the palm of my hand, like a disease, the animal was palpitating, sudden squirms, thrashing, but time went by and the hen hadn't died yet. Taking life isn't easy. I must have made a small, shallow cut, and the animal was suffering, a long and cruel agony. Carla called to me from the other side of the door, without even opening it partway.

"What's happening?"

"Go away."

"Are you mad at me?"

"No."

"Do you want me to help?"

"No."

"Afterwards make sure you clean up."

"Okay."

What kind of a horrible situation had I gotten myself into? I didn't dare step away, the animal might leap up and run wild in the kitchen, spattering everything with blood. But that meant that I had to witness closely the life as it slipped away, the slow process of death that I had triggered. I began to feel an obsessive need to put an end to it, the hen was emitting and smearing a greenish slime all over the marble.

I had taken on a heavy responsibility: to kill, pluck the feathers, strip the yellow body naked, disembowel it, remove the internal organs, and then carefully clean the entire kitchen. I couldn't—I refused to—waste any more time. What is a human being when it kills, what is an animal? What is the difference between slaughtering a beast and murdering a man? Now am I an animal that kills or a man that kills? Is the living creature losing its blood in the sink through my doing really all that different from a human being?

I decided to make the gash larger, make the hen die as quickly as possible. I gripped its neck firmly and pressed down on the knife blade; I could feel the resistance of the cartilage, of the bone structure. The animal thrashed its tightly bound legs, shook its head, its comb, and emitted more greenish goo, closing and opening its terrorized eye. It screamed, a true and horrifying scream that overwhelmed me. Enough, enough, enough, I started to saw at the hen's neck. Just as with the eel years before, I felt an urgent need to separate the head from the body. Deprive the living eye of the possibility of seeing, of seeing me. Separate the brain from the rest of the body as if this would free the victim from the horror, and free us as well. Finally, I hurled the head into the sink, along with the knife.

Carla asked from the hallway: "Did you hurt yourself?"

"No."

"Did you do it?"

"Yes."

"Good job."

Good job. You did a good job of shedding blood. In order to eat. In order to occupy someone else's land. To defend yourself. To drive off invaders. To defend sources of water or oil wells. To conquer sources of water or oil wells. All of these things on this huge verminous ball that day and night a malevolent scarab beetle rolls through a vicious circle, an obtusely fixed orbit in which war follows upon war, massacre follows massacre, and genocide is succeeded by fresh genocide. I carefully swept the balcony, raising clouds of luminous dust. Then I briskly went back to the telephone, and looked up the number of the Hotel Hassler in the phone book.

"Room 317."

"Who do you want?"

"Room 317."

"The name, if you please."

"I beg your pardon?"

"Your name, first of all, and the name of the person with whom you wish to speak."

I hung up.

I couldn't remember if we ever actually ate the chicken, Carla and I. I definitely never tasted the big-headed eels that I hacked to pieces so many years ago, so long ago that remembering that time is like remembering a dream; their snakelike flesh repelled me. The European eel, female despite the fact that the word *capitone* is masculine in Italian, is a lazy eel. It never leaves fresh water, it doesn't swim to the sea, it doesn't cross the Atlantic Ocean to reach the Sargasso Sea, an inferno of fecundity, to lay its eggs there. The eel had already followed that route when it was young, and now it refuses to enter that cycle, it rejects action. The machine that is designed to engender the young has seized up. A senseless but overwhelming force drives most eels to repeat the journey of their mothers, swimming for years from the Sargasso Sea across the boundless Atlantic, to transform themselves as they grow into translucent little eels as thin as leaves, to swim up rivers and rapids and populate in the form of eels the lakes of Europe. Back and forth, back and forth, teeming hordes, first violet, later greenish black, commuters of the blind life force. An obtuse effort in an absurdly repetitive device. The capitone eel refuses, it won't go, it prefers the tooth-studded teeming masses of the muddy ponds, it won't swim thousands of miles to lay its eggs, it suffocates the impulse to give life by dying, and fattens itself up until it winds up beneath the knife. Even so, nothing changes, it's all equally senseless. Both the journey toward the Sargasso Sea and the rejection of that journey end in death. And so?

I carried a chair out onto my balcony. I had grown old without understanding, and there was nothing to understand. In the final analysis all that mattered was the warm March breeze, springtime, the light striking the wall across the way, the consoling colors that conceal the indecipherable nature of the world.

A stream of images—actual, fantastical, dreamed, and remembered. A word, fired by the vocal cords out through the mouth, in a volley of sounds: gutturals, palatals, dentals, labials, nasals. Conciliatory sounds and signs. Or perhaps not, perhaps conversation does not reconcile, does not pacify, does not keep company. We use handsome words to record ugly things, we agree on plans of attack, ambushes, mockeries, genocide, destruction-reconstruction-destruction. We speak violence and we call it the quest for food, hunting, caste, class, competition, market forces, liberation, and new world order. Perhaps the culminating horror is the seed of the words that describe it. An eel sets out for the Sargasso Sea. Or it refuses to do so, and lingers behind in a body of fresh water. But the eel doesn't talk about it, it doesn't orchestrate a melody of words, it names no names, it doesn't reflect upon its decision, it doesn't know what a decision is. But I know, and I am here now. I know, and I tell the story, that I have killed eels, as well as a hen. I did it and, while I was doing it, the hen and the eel experienced their own butchering in every nerve of their bodies without describing to themselves the excruciating pain, without saying to themselves "I am dying," while I did, the whole time I told myself: I am killing. The horror lies in my words: without words, every living thing is convulsion. I am a talking animal, just like in the fables. I am the animal that butchers, flays, dismembers, and all the while recounts; I exterminate and as I do, I mix blood with verbs. I am the animal that creates religion and poetry and history and philosophy and science and psychoanalysis in every corner of the planet, operating from my ever-increasing ability to destroy, and from my tenderhearted determination to destroy the destroyers. I am this body of the beast, with a red tongue that licks and talks. Ah, to be able to rip one's voice from one's throat. To learn silence. To caress one hand with the other.

Night had fallen, I went inside.

14

The next day, I left the apartment at nine thirty in the morning with the pistol and the photograph in my over-coat pocket. I didn't get far though, I immediately turned back. I went upstairs to my apartment, rummaged through the tool drawer unconcernedly, methodically. I was looking for an old switchblade knife from the Forties that I had inherited from my father. It was in the bottom of the drawer, wrapped in an unused sheet of sandpaper. I snapped open the blade, I tested its sharpness, and I put it in my trouser pocket. I felt like a college student who thinks to himself: I'm definitely not going to take my Greek exam; but just in case I decide to do so on the spur of the moment, I want to make sure that I have my identity card with me, my university grade booklet, my notes for a last-minute refresher, pens, pencils, erasers.

I went back downstairs and out into the street, I walked to the bus stop. Outside was, to summarize briefly, the blue of the sky, the green of the trees, the red of the stoplight, the dark-blue of the socks in my black shoes, a swarm of gnats, the lazy flapping of faded banners upon which was written "peace," a cat pouncing outside the gate, passersby hurrying or ambling past, the greenery of the park that extends over the walls and comes dangerously close to putting out your eye, the cars, the buses, a glittering airplane, the thumping helicopter blades like the ones you hear on days when protest marches are going on, with yelling and street fights. I liked every component of the world, when examined in a brief summary.

The bus took me as far as Villa Borghese. From there I continued on foot, ambling casually along Via di Porta Pinciana. I admired the towering pine trees, the oleanders beyond the wall, the languid cypress trees, the palms with their spreading fronds, even the grey of the asphalt, and the cars. Every so often I'd stop in front of a store or in front of an advertising poster. I wasted a little time at Villa Malta, comparing blankly the glittering brass plaque of some corporation or other, on the right-hand pilaster, with the blackened metal of the plaque of the Jesuit monthly *La Civiltà Cattolica*, on the left-hand pilaster. All I really cared about though was killing time; I never actually saw a thing, I saw only my own thoughts. What is a man on his way to commit murder? Let's say I use this pistol. I get out of bed in the morning, I wash up, just like in the diaries I was obliged to keep in elementary school. I eat breakfast while reading the newspaper or listening to the radio. I arm myself, I leave the house. If I have time, I might even drop by the post office to pay an electric bill. My heart has slowed almost to a complete stop, I feel remote.

Or maybe not. The killer's heart beats hard. The killer hasn't slept, or at least I haven't. I thought all night long about someone I knew, someone I spent a few days with during summer holidays, in the country, when I was young. He was an intelligent young man, a law student. His name was Silvio. Once we had talked a whole morning away, while hunting for mushrooms in a chestnut grove, about the possible meanings of Kafka's *Metamorphosis*. Reading that book had confused him, the story struck him as—he used this word—impassable. The expression was striking, it wasn't the sort of word you hear used to describe works of literature. Everything—it emerged—absolutely everything that he had read by Kafka seemed impassable to him. And so I got a little worked up and responded: do you want to resurface Kafka, you want to pave him, put a nice asphalt surface on Kafka? The sort of heated arguments young men have, challenging one another at every occasion. With the passage of time, I became a high school teacher, and he became a policeman. One morning, two young man knocked at his front door. Silvio opened the door, and one of the two shot him in the face.

I remember my reaction when I heard the news of that shooting. I was distraught, I had difficulty breathing. The young man with whom I had discussed Kafka thirteen or fourteen years before now lay on the ground, in a pool of blood, a bullet wound in his face. I felt stunned, not just in my head, but stunned in my hands, my legs, my eyes. All the same, as if I were assigning an element of blame to the victim, I immediately thought: even before he finished university, he thought like a law enforcement officer. That's what I thought, those exact words: law enforcement officer. Before he was shot, I had often thought about him, remembering him as a law student, curious but without much of a sensibility for what literature he had read after reading Franz Kafka; he wondered, and he would ask me, openly, in a mixture of genuine interest and irony: what does this stuff mean, how do I make sense out of it, explain it to me. After the shooting, after I heard the news—I remembered his words: it's impassable, I find Kafka disturbing, he has a paradoxical view of the law. And those phrases, in my mind, were immediately transformed, in my head, into: oh that's why they shot him, he didn't like impassable worlds, even back then he was a law enforcement officer. We'd taken long walks together, we had exchanged ideas and argued about them, we were a couple of twenty-year-olds, before life defined us, endowing us with loves, children, jobs. Now I envision, in flashes, the killers walking up the stairs, the chestnut trees, the understory of the woods, Silvio with dark-brown hair, olive skin, flashing eyes, who hears a knock at the door; perhaps he'd just finished drinking his coffee. But all that flashed into my mind was this: even then, it was clear that he was a law enforcement officer. So in my mind, in a confused, jumbled manner, I drew a link between the motives of the men who shot him, who certainly had no patience with a bourgeois system of laws, and the annoyance that Silvio had expressed for anyone, even Franz Kafka, who made the world impassable.

Why? Why did I think this way?

Because I understood the reasons that can lead someone, in all honesty, adhering to a sort of absolute purity, to shoot a man bright and early in the morning. We can shoot a man, while he is still in his pajamas, because his sense of the law is different from ours, because he finds it objectionable that the law books used in Kafka's *The Trial* are filled with obscenities, because he believes that democracy works fine the way it is and need not be pushed and strained until it becomes a genuine democracy, because, in other words, he believes that the existing system should always and in every case be defended, while we think that the existing system should be torn down— yes! yes! yes!—torn down and sown with salt. When the bullet tore through Silvio's face, I had become a good teacher, a good father, I never broke a law, I was even a scrupulous and impeccable motorist. His terrible fate left me distraught, I remembered the strong handshake of a young man, an open honest smile. But I also thought, as I still think today, that an evil power forces millions and millions of human beings into unacceptable living conditions and that the world we live in is unjust and corrupt down to every last ganglion, and that it is therefore necessary to make a decision—either we rise up and truly take on that evil power in a pitched battle, or else we are complicit, we are no longer innocent. And so, in the flash of a few seconds, I had identified more with the motivations of the terrorist squad than I had sympathized with the young man I had once known.

I checked my watch, it was 10:25 A.M. I walked into a café, ordered an espresso, and spooned a lot of sugar into it. I heard a man of about forty, well dressed, saying to another, with a restrained note of fury in his voice: "What do I have to do, just tell me what I have to do." I couldn't understand the rage of the well-to-do, it disgusted me. It had been easy, thirty years ago, to remove myself from any and all possible affinities with the young people of notable family or promising talent who had carried their surnames to the protest marches, the rallies, the terror wars. Their treacherous murders struck me as yet another exercise of power, I thought that their bold willingness to shed the blood of others was simply a natural extension of their class arrogance. I felt closer to those who were nobodies, those who harbored the hatreds intrinsic to poverty, childhoods spent with the constant danger of abuse, mistreatment, the eyes that had seen in their parents and grandparents the trembling sense of vulnerabilitiy, the humiliation of being in the boss's power, doing the labor on the edge of subsistence that holds you down, until the day you die, in drab routine, you, your family, your children, your grandchildren. With those people, even now, I felt an affinity, even when their murderous deeds were deplorable, cowardly, and what counted most, easily subject to manipulation. It struck me that they were my future. Sooner or later I'd have to chose. And if I failed to choose, they would choose—years from now, decades from now—my daughters, my grandchildren. The world was moving in that odious but inevitable direction toward which they had already begun to move, in the grip of a fever, rather than just sitting and watching. Human beings of all ages were devastated by ferocious exploitation, bombs, torture. Before the indifference of the well-to-do, men, women, and children, driven by the despair of poverty and hunger, hurried by the thousands to drown in the sea just off our coasts, our homes. Everyone, eventually, would be forced to decide not whether or not to shed blood, but which blood to shed: the blood of the oppressed or the blood of the oppressors. When I realized that I was thinking this intolerable thought, I tossed back the last bit of espresso in my cup. Yes, the whole planet was up in arms. The most peaceable place imaginable, this café filled with well-fed, well-dressed people, for instance, could be transformed in the space of an instant, while the gears of the wall clock were counting out their last second, into a blot of dead and dying flesh. Every individual, to an ever greater degree, would become a carrier of destruction, a device made of flesh that could be activated at the drop of a hat.

Like me, for instance.

I looked at my reflection in the mirror behind the bar. I was an elderly man, pale, skinny, soberly dressed. There was nothing about me that gave away the fact that I had a pistol and a knife in my pocket. I felt as if I represented a kind of twofold normality: the normality of life's daily habits in a secure western city, and the normality of the executions about which we read every day in the newspapers and we hear about on TV.

I paid, I left the café, and I walked up Via Gregoriana. Hand-made shoes. Yellow and violet dishes. Ferdinand Gregorovius lived here. Palazzo Tomati, XVIII century. Treats for the idle eye. What does a killer do? A killer thinks about his victim, thumbs through the principal reasons why he is willing to kill, eggs himself on with his slogans, reviews the code that he has learned over time, a code that helps to keep everything inside him from going askew. Or perhaps he goes directly to his target without a second thought, without imagination, dead set on his hatreds, principles, the need to shed blood, and even enjoys the growing sense of tension throughout his body. Perhaps a killer, at each step along the way, is able to persuade himself that his victims are not really human beings. Or that they are human beings of a poorly developed, unsuccessful sub-species. Or else that they are nothing more than silhouettes in a larger shooting range. Or that they are enemies, a classification familiar from our childhood games. Or perhaps that they are indeed humans, humans who must be killed not out of hatred but in order that the cause may be victorious, that revenge be exacted, that a filthy informer be punished, that a stain be cleansed in blood, or that a threat be averted. The killer, perhaps, never really feels that he is naked in the presence of the person whom he is about to strike down. He always wears a thick uniform. He is a traitor, a fraud. He's a hired killer. He's a Mafioso, a Camorrista. He's a Fascist. He's a Red Brigades terrorist. He's a suicide bomber who will kill, at the same time dying in the name of God. Perhaps, I thought, in order to shed blood you must first of all define yourself. I wondered who I was, who I could claim to be. I discovered with a sense of disquiet that I couldn't think of anything to cling to. I was full of information, analysis, arguments, and predictions, but I was entirely devoid of any genuine affiliation. I had learned over the years, without any particular shockwaves to affect the routines of my daily life and my beliefs, that such-and-such a person had been killed, and then another person, and then someone else after him. The corpses appeared on television, in the newspapers, and then vanished immediately, erased from everyday life, from the interpretative scheme to which I adhered, from the mental schemes I carried with me when I left my home each morning. Now I found it repugnant to think of placing the names of all the victims in a chain, one after the other, it would have been too frightening, I would have wondered: is it possible? Is it possible that all this took place during the space of my working existence? Did I have anything to do with it or not? I was certainly not responsible for the actual killings. How could I, for instance, have killed Vittorio Bachelet? How could I have killed Riccardo Palma or Ezio Tarantelli? How could I have climbed the stairs, knocked on the front door, and fired a gun into the face of someone with whom I had once had a conversation about Kafka? These were harmless human beings. They held things to them, they said words, they walked to and fro. They read books, studied, led middle-class lives. They weren't armed. And even if they had been, death came for them by surprise, their minds were so unconcerned with any mortal danger that they never had the chance to react. Ah, the horror of the violated bodies! A person should always wonder: could I have done it? I thought about it the whole distance of my walk, with the taste of the coffee still in my mouth.

No, I couldn't have done it.

Or maybe yes, I could have done it.

It can be. It can be done.

I found—or I felt as if I'd found—confirmation in the position I had assumed: if they shot him, it's because he was a law enforcement officer. It was sufficient to formulate that equation, hammer it down with a good solid nail, use it as indicator of our own personal rectitude, and we would be able to find our way through the chaos of the world: men of the old order, men of the new order. It was sufficient for each sentence to follow the last, and they could render superfluous both living bodies and concrete things. And in the meanwhile, continue to forge a chain of words, each word a link, connecting to the hand that once decapitated an eel, a hen from which to make dinner, a hand that had experienced the taking of life without tossing away the knife in disgust and turning to vomit in a corner of the kitchen.

I could shoot, yes, even without entirely committing myself, even without being a member of this militant formation or that terrorist group. In the end, it is the mere everyday distortion—the distortion of justice, of right actions, of a fair life, the distortion of lives in pursuit of profit—that arms the hand and the desperation of the individual. I arrived at the Hotel Hassler at a quarter to eleven.

15

I entered through the revolving door. I wanted to look like a jaded expert who knows what he's doing and where he's going; I wanted to look like an habitué of five-star hotels. Beyond that, however, I had no plan. I was there because Nina had asked me to go to an apartment in Via Pavia. I had gone there, but the way you might go to the home of a friend on vacation to water his plants. I had diligently transcribed a quotation from a book, I had passed it on to a stranger, I had received a package that contained a pistol and a photograph. Someone had made an appointment for me, and I had arrived a little ahead of schedule. Here I was then, on the top of the Spanish Steps, in the lobby of the Hotel Hassler, dim yellow lights, on the right a she-wolf suckling Romulus and Remus, on the left, the conciergerie, the cash registers, the reception desk. I asked the desk clerk, coughing a fake cough:

"Is Doctor Pah-*hrumph*, pardon me! in his room—Room 317?"

"Who should I say?"

"Stasi."

The desk clerk smiled: "Professor Stasi?"

"That's right."

"Good morning, Professor. Just a moment."

As he called upstairs to Room 317, I tried to control my surprise. So, I was expected. Or perhaps someone had just left my name, and even my profession. What was the point of that? What else should I expect?

I distractedly followed with my gaze a pair of hotel employees who were carrying an elegant gilt metal easel and setting it up close to the entrance. It looked like a sign announcing a show of some kind, or else a conference or a lecture. From where I was sitting it was difficult to read. People entered and people left: tourists, businessmen. The desk clerk said: "The Maestro isn't in his room."

Maestro? maestro of what? You need only grow old practicing any given art with a middling mastery and you became a "maestro." I nodded, said thank you, tried to think of anything to say that might obtain a little information about the man in Room 317 and why my name was familiar at the hotel conciergerie. I was afraid that I'd say the wrong thing, somehow, so I asked only:

"May I wait for him here?"

"Please, make yourself comfortable."

Absentmindedly I stroked the back of the she-wolf, attracted primarily by a gleam on the deep black metal. Display windows with jewelry, purses, shoes, gloves. I looked around: at the far end was an even more dimly lit hall, and the silhouette of a piano. I tried to find a place where I could keep an eye on the entrance and, at the same time, the desk clerk. I couldn't find one, so I cautiously moved an easy chair into position. I sat down, stared at the brightly lit display case in front of me, with delicately colored jewelry. For years I had experienced dark spots dancing before my eyes like flies; I looked around for a less brightly lit corner. I waited.

Little by little the wave of lassitude that had brought me there began to abate. I put my hand in my pocket, I felt the photograph and pistol, and the physical contact made my head spin. Perhaps a still-silent cancer was taking up residence in my brain. My thyroid, I thought: is that the source of this sort of blind emotion that brought me to this place, this lobby? I should phone Sellitto. I was a victim of a hardening of the arteries, my former student had warned me, he had said: Professor, if you need anything, phone me. An admirable young man, not like Nina: a guardian of law and order who still had time to worry about the mental health of his old Italian teacher. Why had I been so acquiescent? Why was I continuing to be compliant; why didn't I ask the desk clerk, clearly: "Who is waiting for me? Who left my name here? Who is the man in Room 317?" Why shouldn't I show him the photograph in my pocket, why not ask him: is this the Maestro?

I removed my glasses, I rubbed my eyelids. I already knew the answer. I was there out of a mental habit dating back decades, in order to reassure myself that I was me, that I was allied with a dark, living mass, traveling against the stream across oceans, rivers, across the planet. I couldn't feel any bond with a person who could afford to stay in a hotel like this, located in one of the most beautiful places on the planet. Even the few times I had stayed in a place like this with Carla, I had felt guilty. Comfort, luxury, the pleasure of enjoying a lavish holiday, the enjoyment of beauty was still, to me at the age of almost seventy, were all forms of treason.

Through the main entrance of the hotel a man entered, moving slowly, limping slightly, heavyset, perfectly bald, with a pale puffy face. It was the man from the photograph. He headed for the dark cornice behind which the desk clerk smiled deferentially.

The clerk pointed in my direction, and the new arrival glanced over at me for a second or two, motionless. I stood up, and he began limping in my direction. He smiled, displaying a mouthful of bright white false teeth; I could hear his labored breathing.

"How are you doing?"

I shook his hand, it was clammy with sweat: "Fine."

"Sit down."

I sat down, and he sat down as well with a prolonged groan, and then looked at me, uncertainly: "You don't recognize me, do you?"

He gave me plenty of time to examine him, staring at me all the while with his ironic eyes, suffocated by the heavy eyelids, and the puffy circles beneath them. He understood that I wasn't kidding him, I really had no idea who he was, and he burst into laughter. At that point, however, his vital, naturally joyous laugh reached me simultaneously from the depth of his barrel chest and the distance of the years. Instantly, his face leapt into my mind as if it had been stripped of flesh, revealing hidden features that restored the physiognomy of long ago.

"Luciano," I murmured, incredulous.

It was Luciano Zara, my Comrade from so many years ago.

16

H ow could it be, I thought, what is Luciano doing here after all this time. But he was already talking with the engaging cordiality he'd always had.

"It's so unfair. Life has consumed me, but it left you as you were."

"You look fine."

"Liar. Look at me: I'm overweight, I drink, eat, and smoke too much. A body needs to be maintained in good condition, like yours."

In a rapid series of phrases he informed me that he suffered from diabetes, that he couldn't manage to take decent care of himself, that no one pushed him to take good care of himself because he answered to no one, no women, no children. The only human bond that he had was with his parents, who were both still alive. He exclaimed:

"It's all their fault that I don't pay attention to my health and I live like a reckless young man. It's hard to believe that you're truly mortal, if your mother and father refuse to die."

"I have a few things wrong with me."

"Like what?"

"A problem with my thyroid."

"It certainly doesn't show, you look perfect, your neck doesn't sag, not even a bit."

He was always eager to talk, one of those people that if you give them a slight push, they start telling stories. The only thing that had changed, I noticed immediately, was that now he spoke without the frankness, the spirited warmth that used to characterize his conversation. Now he was chilly, each of his phrases rang like barbed wire in an icy field. He started off on the disappointment of his parents. The two old people really treated him as if he were still a little boy, they kept pestering him, telling him that he could have done so much more with his life. His father had been a professor of economics at the University of Bari, and an important one; his mother was an outstanding biologist who worked at a hospital. They had raised him well; his mother had given him his love for the piano. He had graduated from university at the age of twenty-one, he was a gifted young man, and he could easily have remained in academia if he had wanted to.

"We were just reckless fools," he said disgustedly, "we wasted our time and that's all we did. We thought: everything now! Instead, everything you achieve is the result of patient work, negotiation, mediation, one small step after another. Isn't it?"

"I don't know about that. You see what a disaster we've created by taking small steps? Widespread corruption, a left wing that's impossible to tell apart from the right, thieves, wars, the ones on top remain in command and the ones at the bottom stay there. There's not a single place on the planet where justice determines people's lives."

"You're still harping on that point?"

"What else should I care about?"

"Reality."

"And what is reality?"

"It's consuming, food and oneself—getting fat, changing, getting worse, coping every day with that which exists."

"What exists is atrocious."

"Okay, I see, you never grew up."

"I'm not sure if growing up is such a wonderful thing."

"What's wonderful, my dear man, is to understand that this life of ours is what exists, here, now, and nothing more."

It had come to him all of a sudden one day. He had wasted all that time believing the flames were at the gates, that the time was ripe, that the primary condition would converge with the secondary conditions and: wham bam, the new order would arrive. Nonsense. He had done his best to make up for lost time, he had worked for a while with the Italian Socialists. He had quit working as a teacher, he had moved to Milan, he had found a nice little position at the university. Things had gone nicely. He had even obtained political posts of a certain importance. Then had come the period when all the turds floated to the surface, a period of slowdown, a natural part of the cycle, but in the mid-Nineties he had become a consultant—what kind of consultant?—and he'd recovered lost ground. In the last decade he'd done very nicely indeed. He said that by now he no longer gave a crap about all the so-called political idiocy, the splendor or the misery of the times, depending on the daily pronouncements of the newspapers or the television. But he was a great admirer of the economist and cabinet minister Giulio Tremonti, for a certain period he had been a member of Tremonti's staff.

I sat there listening to him, trying to sense behind or beneath his words any trace of guilt.

I was increasingly mystified, I could feel a growing sense of humiliation, I was unable to grasp what was happening. When Nina was my student, Luciano had already stopped being a teacher many years before. So why had she and her friends sent me here? Why did they want to punish him? What role does this man play in their symbolic universe? Do they want to kill him because he worked for the Socialists? Isn't it a little late to be worrying about that now? Do they want to kill him because, let's say, he worked for small-scale manufacturing in Lombardy? Then why down here in Rome instead of up north in Milan? Did they put this pistol in my pocket because he was once a revolutionary and now he admired a former finance minister from a center-right coalition government? That makes no sense. He's not well known, who could possibly know about him? Until just a few minutes ago, I didn't even know what he had done with his life.

"And what have you done in all these years?"

"What I've always done. I taught. Now I'm retired."

"And do you still study and study, even at night?"

"Yes."

"Without ever learning a thing though."

"That may be."

"No, my dear man, it's mathematical. It's enough to look at your face, it's sufficient to look at the clothing you have on, your shoes."

"I don't study to understand things, I study to keep myself company."

"So it's a kind of hobby."

"Yes."

"Like the piano for me."

"Yes."

He laughed in his contagious manner, and then returned to his list of regrets. If he hadn't kept his love of music to himself, he might have become a truly great musician. I made mistakes, he said. Late in life, he had decided to perform in public, but only at the end of the Eighties. Now he did it to amuse himself, he played for his friends. "But the minute I sense that the audience is restless, I stop playing and leave," he exclaimed.

I listened closely, it seemed as if a little passion had begun to stir in his voice. Every so often, I asked myself, almost in amusement: was I sent here because he plays the piano nicely? Is that what he's guilty of? What kind of a mess is this? Is this a revenge killing on behalf of one of his old girlfriends?

I smiled.

"What is it?"

"Do you remember Nadia?"

"Who's that?"

"The girl whose apartment you sent me to, to pick up a suit-case of yours. It was, let's see, 1976."

"I don't remember a thing, it's all vanished."

"You don't even remember when you had a fever and you came to stay at my house?"

"That I remember. Did this Nadia have something to do with it?"

"Yes."

"What's happened with your daughters?"

"The girls have jobs. One has an only son, the other one has two daughters. The elder girl is divorced, the young one is about to divorce."

"And your wife?"

"She died last year."

We said nothing, but only for a few seconds. Then he made a sweeping gesture:

"Other times."

"Yes."

"I saved your family."

"In what sense."

He burst into laughter, a certain caustic tone returned in his voice: "In every sense: your marriage, your domestic tranquility, the happiness of your daughters. I left and I saved you."

I looked at him. What was he telling me? My marriage, my domestic tranquility, the happiness of my daughters. I didn't want to hear it, I hoped he wouldn't say anything else. But the damage was done. Whether Luciano kept talking or said nothing more, whether he explicitly explained his reference, or limited himself to nudging a faded old suspicion into the realm of almost certainty, everything was—I'm not sure how to put this—shrinking. I left and I saved you. How old had Carla been in 1976, thirty-five, thirty-six? This puffy, swollen man, almost featureless, was manipulating the shadow of my wife in such a way that I could see her as she offered herself to him, and he rejected her. I could sense the elevated sound of those days deflating: the suffering of the planet, hunger, thirst, wars, Iraq, Iran, Afghanistan, the expansion of China and India, the struggle of the oppressed peoples, political violence, and arms and weapons. Thoughts that suddenly became irrelevant. His tawdry words had made the blood pound in my temples. Is that why I had a pistol in my pocket? Was I about to use a gun because of a subtle phrase that was apparently a statement of friendship and loyalty?

"Have something to drink," he urged me as if, after hearing his words, I needed a strong shot of alcohol.

"No, thanks."

I stood up.

"What, you're going away? Are you upset about something?"

"No, of course not."

"You'll come back for the concert, I hope."

"What concert?"

"I'm performing this evening."

"Here?"

He stood up, too, took my arm, and led me over to the gilt metal easel. It held an elegant poster board, announcing his concert.

"Look, you see how big the name is? It's tonight, at eleven: try to come if you can, we'll have dinner together. Don't play tricks on me, heh heh, that's the last thing I need. That's why you called, isn't it? I reserved a table just for you. It's a dinner party with friends of mine: writers, intellectuals, people who still think they count for something, but who don't mean a damn thing. I'm performing Franz Liszt. Do you like his *Nuages Gris*? You know I never boast, but my execution of that piece leaves people just speechless."

I realized that my right hand was plunged into my pocket, wrapped tightly around the grip of my pistol.

Execution.

Execution of the *Nuages Gris*, Hotel Hassler, at 11 P.M., cancel.

The sense of humiliation became intolerable.

I murmured: "All right, I'll try to make it."

17

As far as I was concerned, the story could have ended there. Sure it was still pretty rough, I needed to do some work on it, the necessary elements to make it all add up weren't there yet. But I was tempted to bring the story to an end with that "all right, I'll try to make it."

According to my plan—though it might be excessive to speak of a plan, really it is more appropriate to speak of pictures and voices—I still had a few chapters to write. I wanted to bring Nina back onstage, use her for a sort of epilogue. Or a prologue: I'd decide later, often things that are written for the end wind up being placed at the beginning. My intention was to shift brusquely over to Stasi's former student, slip into her head, and change her from the icy third person she had been at the beginning, into a first person with anxieties, uncertainties, sudden surges of determination, and obscure regions of the soul. But was that necessary? Couldn't I arrange to have Stasi say, in a few dolorous lines, that which had not yet been made clear?

I decided to take some time, try to gather my thoughts. I went to France for work, I came back to Rome, I wrote a preface for the Italian edition of John Fante's *Dago Red*. But the professor, like a disgruntled ghost, refused to step aside to make way for Nina. For all that time, he remained at the Hotel Hassler, in the lobby, his hand wrapped around the grip of his pistol, or perhaps he stepped out into the street, but went no further than the balustrade at the top of the Spanish Steps, the Rampa Mignanelli.

One morning—I was alone in the apartment—Mina called me again. I had succeeded in forgetting about that unpleasant story, just thinking about it made me anxious. As soon as I recognized the woman's heavy voice, the blood rushed to my head.

"You again?"

"I've read your books, Professor. Before all this, I'd never even heard of you, and then I said to myself: let me see what kind of books this fellow writes."

"Listen, I have work to do, pardon me, but I have to hang up now."

"I just wanted to tell you one thing: you, in your book *Via Gemito*, attribute the responsibility for the death of your mother from cirrhosis of the liver to your father, do you remember?"

"And so?"

"And so, in that book you describe how a person can trigger a disease in the body of another, or have you forgotten?"

"Signora, *Via Gemito* is a novel, and novelists invent things, they exaggerate."

Silence. Then the woman said in a pained voice, full of suffering: "We are poor people, Professor, but we'll take this to the limit. We have lots of witnesses to what happened on that bus. If our father dies, we'll take this up with a lawyer. Whatever it costs us."

"Do whatever you think best."

"Yes, and I want to tell you this: I am a devout Catholic, Jesus comes before anything else for me, so I have forgiven you. So has my husband. But my brother hasn't, he's incapable of it. He believes in an eye for an eye, a tooth for a tooth. If we turn to the courts, it won't be to do you any harm, but only to prevent my brother from seeking justice in the wrong way."

My anger suddenly collapsed.

Up till then I had felt certain that this woman was trying to squeeze money out of me, threatening family vendettas or senseless lawsuits; suddenly I sensed a genuine concern in her voice, as if in her delirium she were trying to warn me of a genuine danger, not just for me, but for her family as well, and so lawyers and a court of law were not a threat, but the only peaceful solution available in a situation of fury and grief and ferocious blame. A way of saving us all.

"Mina," I mumbled, "I'm not a wealthy man, quite the contrary, I don't know what you imagine. Let me talk to your husband, with your brother, we'll come to an understanding."

She shot back: "Right now that's impossible, Professor, our father is a very sick man. I pray for everyone's well-being that he doesn't die. Goodbye."

I immediately went to see a friend of mine who is a lawyer, to hear his professional opinion. He just laughed and told me that I faced no legal risk. I mean, he exclaimed, laughing, if I call you a son of a bitch to your face, and you die six months later of liver cancer, am I legally responsible for your death? He recommended that I go to the police. In fact, he added, if there are any more phone calls, make sure to record them. In conclusion, he said, these people are trying to scare a little money out of you. Times are hard, poverty is everywhere, people get by as best they can. I thanked him and felt a little better.

But I never went to the police. Then and there, I had thought of going to see my former student, the one who carried a pistol in her purse even to go eat in a pizzeria, and tell her everything, ask her for advice. But then it occurred to me that Mina and her relatives might really be penniless. Savings squandered on useless treatment for their father, victims of unscrupulous physicians. The squalor of disease, of pain. I gradually began to feel guilty for having considered taking legal steps to protect myself from them. I had a growing feeling of pain in my heart, a sense of remorse. I remembered what happened on the bus, I remembered that I had thumped the man repeatedly against the closed exit door. I was gripping him by the lapel, and I had dragged him out of the bus the instant the doors swung open. To attack the helpless, fragile people, terrified by the rapid, overwhelming changes in society: I would never have done such a thing when I was younger, what a deplorable situation. I had certainly done the right thing by defending the black woman, there could be no question about that. But what drove me to take it beyond the limit? I remembered Stasi. Perhaps he resisted leaving the stage because he wanted to go beyond a certain limit as well, and I was preventing him from doing so. Or maybe he was doing everything within his power to keep from crossing that line and I couldn't understand that and the story seemed to be over, but in reality I was just stuck, I didn't know how to take it to its logical conclusion.

One afternoon I reread the last few lines and started to rewrite, just to see what would happen. The professor realized that his right hand was wrapped around the pistol grip. Execution, he thought. Execution of Franz Liszt's *Nuages Gris*, Hotel Hassler, at eleven o'clock, cancel. What did that mean? Had they sent him there to listen to a concert but instead of specifying A.M. or P.M., they had simply written eleven o'clock? Was he simply supposed to listen to a piano solo by Liszt, and thus learn to be a placid old man? Or had he simply come at the wrong time? Was he supposed to shoot Comrade Luciano that evening? Feeble questions, devoid of anguish, in fact slightly ironic in tone. Stasi sensed that he had wandered into a trap, but not into the most obvious one. What was hemming him in on all sides was not the police, but the few treacherous phrases uttered by Luciano and the diabolical shift of the word execution from redemptive violence to the musical art of the *Nuages Gris*. He felt as if every cell in his body was evaporating from the oppressive heat. He reddened, he was suffocating. The problem—the danger—was that in the space of a few seconds everything was shriveling, losing all dignity. The thing to do now was beat a hasty retreat, before the blood surged to his head like a column of lava. He murmured: "All right, I'll try to make it." He wanted to turn and walk toward the exit, but he couldn't bring himself to do it. The motivations that had driven him to this point had shrunk. The magnanimous wave of youth, never fully straddled and engaged, restrained for an entire lifetime, now finally was yearning to break and crash down in a foaming miserable explosion of jealous fury. How evanescent is the boundary between elevated altruistic motives and the most vile, self-interested ones. The conceited phrase uttered by Zara, that large, puffy man, ready to do a bit of evil with a smile to anyone who happened within reach, continued to echo in his head like a horrible auditory hallucination.

I saved your family.

Stasi looked over at the revolving door a few yards away— his escape route—but he couldn't see anything else, he couldn't *see*, that's the exact term, anything other than the heft of the weapon in his pocket, and it struck him as the only antidote to humiliation.

Let's accept, he thought, that the insinuation has no basis in reality, that it's just one of Luciano's cruel boasts, a mind game, a display of false loyalty, isn't it still a ferocious attack on my love for Carla?

He took a step toward the door—already Luciano had turned his back to him, and was walking toward the dark counter where the desk clerk stood—but it suddenly struck him as cowardly just to leave. Shame was weighing him down, making him feel almost hunchbacked, as if it were the pommel of the cane upon which Luciano was leaning with all his weight as he limped back to the conciergerie. And yet, at the same time, it only fed his rage. Everything, all around him, was moving slowly and tumultuously, both ponderous and volatile. The weapon felt like a weight that his fingers could no longer support, the pocket of his overcoat was a deep well.

Luciano reached the counter, turned to repeat his cordial invitation to Stasi: "Till this evening, okay, I hope to see you," and Stasi nodded in the affirmative, and as he did he saw Luciano raise his arm in a sarcastic clenched-fist salute.

The professor had never given that salute on any occasion in his entire life; his sense of the ridiculous had kept him from doing so. But now that the ridiculous hemmed him in on all sides, something incongruous happened inside him, something that is difficult to put into words. For an instant he saw Carla, he saw the girls, he saw the Communists raising their fists with dignity as they faced the firing squad, and in the time it took Luciano to turn, laughing, back toward the desk clerk, he felt a sudden urgent need to defend the symbolism behind that clenched-fist salute—everything that it contained—against Luciano's uncontrollable impulse to mock everything. He pulled his gun out of his pocket, held his arm straight out, as rigid as he could. He held his hat in the other hand, by the brim. He squeezed off one shot, then two.

But nothing happened. Luciano's large body had no reaction other than to turn rapidly on its axis, driven by curiosity at the sound of gunfire, while the clerk on the far side of the counter, who was able to see Stasi and understood that he was armed, stood open-mouthed—in wonder and terror.

The professor continued to fire, and still Luciano showed not the slightest sign of falling, nor did blood appear on his overcoat or shirt, nor was there any other sign of imminent death. Then Stasi realized that there was no way of putting an end to his humiliation.

There were no more bullets.

The gun went off, with small, harmless, flashing explosions, like guns that I had owned as a child, guns that fired paper caps or flash cartridges.

I worked for a couple of hours, but half-heartedly. I had decided to take Stasi right up to the moment in which he finally fires his gun, in part to give his repressed violence an outlet of some kind, and in part so that he could discover that the gun was loaded with blanks. But I found it improbable that he would fire, just like that, concealing a long-simmering jealousy behind a theoretical defense of the clenched-fist salute. Already, even as I was writing, I had begun to harbor another feeling: the professor gathers his strength, he escapes, avoids the trap of irony, manages to keep from being made a laughing-stock, he rescues the substance of his life, and manages to convey his world to safety; but, inevitably, that world deflates like a balloon that a child leaves, round and full, bumping against the ceiling, the night before, only to discover it the next morning on the floor.

That evening, I tried using Stasi's sense of humiliation to give him the strength to make it, in a state of nervous prostration, through the revolving door. The professor realizes that, in his pocket, his right hand is spasmodically wrapped around the grip of his pistol. Execution, he thinks. Execution of Franz Liszt's *Nuages Gris*, then. Here, at the Hotel Hassler, at 11 o'clock. Cancel. Cancel the memory of the last few days. Don't investigate, don't delve into the meaning—the non-meaning, the non-sense—of words and actions, at my age it could be dangerous. He said, under his breath, not really to Luciano, almost to himself: All right, I'll try to make it, and he let go of the pistol grip and stretched out his hand, offering to shake the hand of the old comrade of his youth. But Luciano had already sarcastically raised his arm and now he was giving the clenched-fist salute, another diabolical piece of mockery. Stasi hesitated for an instant, plunged his hand back into his over-coat pocket, then he smiled bitterly and turned to leave, making his way toward the exit at the ponderous gait of an old man on unsteady legs.

Once he made it out of the hotel, he walked down the Spanish Steps, then he headed for the Piazza del Popolo. It didn't feel like a March day, the weather was growing warmer and warmer. The professor walked for a long time without being aware of the street, the people, the cars, until he reached the bus stop in Piazzale Flaminio. He hoped that if he succeeded in getting far away from Luciano, from the phrase "I saved your family," from the ambiguity of the word "execution," from the mocking clenched-fist salute, without dissolving his image as a tranquil elderly professor filled with pronouncements and aches and pains, if he could even thrust back into their dens his feelings of shame and anger, then he would be safe. The 495 bus pulled up, he boarded.

Behind him a very fat black woman boarded the bus, and pressed up against him to get by, to go up the aisle. Go right ahead, ma'am, he said. The woman tried to make her way up the bus aisle to reach the ticket-stamping machine. But a fifty-year-old man began to insult her, saying that she had shoved him rudely. He shouted a string of vulgarities at her, and then started in on anybody that came under the heading of non-European or migrant or any other epithet you care to name.

Stasi felt a painful throbbing in his head, for an instant he imagined the interior of his cranium as a tunnel lit by a long string of light bulbs. He realized that now, far away from the comfortable environment of the Hotel Hassler, enclosed in that tumultuous shard of the world, his entire life really was at risk. The situation might have been confusing in the hotel lobby, but here on the bus it was becoming blinding. A lingering stream of the rage that had arisen in the presence of Luciano was still whirling and tumbling, seeking a more suitable opportunity to burst into full fury. However much he tried to keep his temper, the professor didn't know how to—didn't want to—calm himself down. He lunged forward and said to the man:

"Shut your mouth, you idiot."

"What the fuck do you want?"

"You need to apologize to the lady."

"And you need to go fuck yourself."

"No, you need to go fuck yourself, and fuck your mother and your sister too, you piece of shit. Get out of this bus and say the things you said to that poor woman to me, on the sidewalk. Let's go!"

Stasi realized that he was already pushing him toward the exit door, he wanted to hurl him out onto the sidewalk the second the doors whooshed open and then rush down the steps and grip him furiously by the throat and throttle him until his eyes bulged out of their sockets. He had forgotten who he was, how old he was. Suddenly he was speaking in dialect, a turgid violent Neapolitan dialect. It never entered his mind for a second that the other man could much more easily have done to him what he so urgently needed to do to him. On the contrary, he felt as if he were a furious, disembodied demon. He was certain that even if the man had stabbed him through and through or shot him in the chest, he would have felt nothing, the only thing he understood was the blinding need to kill him.

The man must have seen that burning need in Stasi's eyes, in the determination with which Stasi pushed him toward the exit, in the fury in Stasi's hands. He muttered something, said that Stasi was an old man, so he'd let him live this once. He stepped out of the bus the instant the doors swung open. But Stasi stepped down behind him, he didn't waste a second. The man had turned white as a sheet, he was stepping away from him, walking backwards with footsteps that were alternately clumsy and frantic, his mouth was gaping and closing. He didn't escape immediately, but it struck the professor that in order to get away from him, he was gathering himself together—collecting himself—with all his strength and then splintering himself away heavily, now a leg, now an arm, now the head. It was a weird, off-kilter flight, Stasi kept after him.

He caught up with him near a large street door leading into a monumental building, an entryway with a staircase on the right and another one on the left. Stasi grabbed the man and shoved him into the open lobby. The man seemed unable to speak, he was spluttering, suffocating. The professor trundled him backward until he reached a dimly lit hallway that led to the elevator. He raised the pistol, shoved it in the man's mouth, and fired.

Once, twice.

Nothing happened except that the man sank to his knees, becoming so heavy that Stasi could no longer hold him up; he allowed him to collapse into a seated position on the floor, his head and back against the elevator door.

The professor was astonished but not upset, he looked at the pistol from which a plume of smoke still issued. He had heard the shots, he smelled the cordite, but he could see no blood, the man's throat and skull were still intact, there was only an overwhelming and intolerable smell of shit. Stasi tossed the pistol to one side, calmly rummaged in his overcoat pocket, extracted the knife, and flicked it open. He squatted down and plunged the blade into the man's throat, as the man began struggling, clutching into a ball, convulsing, thrashing. The blade was old, it cut badly, it ground against the cartilage and bone, blood spurted in all directions. Now the professor had one knee braced against the man's chest and he was jerking his head back, hauling on it by a handful of hair. The victim was kicking, trying to ward him off, but his hands had no strength, he was clutching at thin air, he was smacking his open palms against the blood-slick floor or flinging his hands straight up, banging his knuckles against the elevator door. He had to saw his head off, he had to be certain that there would never again be a connection between the brain and the rest of the body. Stasi worked doggedly with his knife until the man's large head tumbled, eyes staring, onto the floor, rolling until it came to a stop in a corner, displaying the nape of the neck to him.

This last version, my wife told me, is definitely abhorrent, you need to delete it.

I justified myself, muttering that I was exploring a series of possibilities. They were rough drafts, I still hadn't decided anything. But she insisted, that possibility needed to be rejected, she preferred that the path of the elderly professor, the force that had pushed him from one station to the next, should remain undecipherable until the end. I said, with irritation: Well, I'll see what I decide to do.

She didn't know anything about the man on the bus, any of what had happened, or about Mina, and so it was difficult, in the specific case, to explain that putting into the story something of what had really happened gave me a sense, on the one hand, of truth, which helped my writing, and on the other gave me a sense of fiction that reassured me in real life.

All the same, the bloody crescendo of the episode soon came to seem excessive to me as well. Was it necessary for Stasi to shoot the man? Did he really have to use the knife too? Hadn't I really pushed the character as far as he could go? Discard all that, go back to the story of Nina. I was even afraid that my hand was being tugged by a sort of professional curiosity for the splatter genre. Already I could envision myself wasting time poring over anatomy textbooks or making phone calls to doctor friends of mine to learn exactly what happens when you cut a human being's throat, if it's possible to sever a living human being's head with an old switchblade knife from the Forties. I decided to opt for restraint, to reel Stasi in, to convince him to sprinkle sugar over his broken world. I returned to the moment when he was taking his leave from Luciano and leaving the Hotel Hassler.

"All right," he said, "I'll try to make it."

He slowly pushes against the handle of the revolving door, he turns and walks toward the Via Sistina. They had really played him for a fool. They had placed him face to face with himself to see what he would do: would he become someone else or would he charge straight at the mirror, shattering it into pieces? He hadn't done either thing, he had stopped just in time, and now he was done with it. Make the best of it—this is the time for that. Sweeten everything, rewrite the past as if he had not been subjected to the kind of willful humiliation that engenders hatred, but merely a cheerful array of nice sentiments.

Little by little he resumed his reactive ways, as he had trained himself to do over the decades. His aches and pains returned, along with other worries, and the tightness in his neck where the physician had palpated his thyroid. He was himself again, none other than himself, with his filamentous nerves, his chemical tides, his moods. He repressed his resentment. He found space for the idea that those who had driven him to that extreme point had done so with only one goal in mind: they wished to educate him to his true identity, and to his surprise he found himself feeling a certain gratitude. No, he was no warrior combatant for Communism. He was no executor of orders in a war that had gone on for too long. Even if he had thought, sometimes, that there was no other way than by taking up arms to open the doors of the Kingdom of Heaven to all the exploited, all the abused people on earth, in fact he had always known that he was incapable of so doing. And now—today—what nonsense: to go to the Hotel Hassler armed with a pistol, breathing heavily, groping blindly, for an execution, him of all people, incapable as he was of shoving hard, leaping or lunging. Even Luciano seemed like a brother to him now, in his old age, in his overweight, diseased organism, in the life that continued to dwindle, like the contrail of an airplane dissolving in the high winds. And Carla. Controlling one's emotions is a difficult thing. Life, if you restrain it too much, becomes impoverished. The demand of absolute faithfulness is like a red-hot blade on the flesh, designed to sear away, in one fell application, all sensibility, all feeling. She had cultivated a certain moderation, she had stayed with him, she had raised the girls, she had kept him at her side with tenderness. The wave of profound emotion continued to swell. He thought of all that his wife had given him, how she had kept him company. What else could he demand of her? Time to go home, immediately. He was a man who for some time now had experienced no real emotions, he limited himself to reliving them with a distant sense of pleasure. He waited for the bus, sunk in a sort of seraphic sentiment of life, what he attributed in his own boyhood to Domenico Savio. Here I am with my hair neatly combed, he thought, the little cravat, the lily in his hands, Don Bosco in the background. At the age of sixty-seven, I've finally done it. I have no more feelings of indignation. I am calm. I need order, this is the truth of my body today, I no longer need disorder. I fear, like everyone in this city, muggings, drug addicts, burglaries, the spread of the Mafia, the litter and filth in the streets, the deterioration of customs, the guilds of the idle and unemployed, the lack of efficiency, the thieving government. But without hysterical pitches, please. No vituperous old age. An old man should practice moderation on a daily basis, the peaceful art of the mediator. I am aware of wrongdoing, certainly—more and more every day—but I have finally learned to address first and foremost the mistakes in the things I do myself. In the murderer I can recognize the possibility that I myself might become one and I can therefore understand his motives, comprehend them, and yet all the same feel horror, and thus recoil.

18

They came to get me at 7:20 in the morning, I remember that before I opened the door I looked at the clock. My father immediately started working to find a lawyer for me: this was the beginning of a horrible period. The interrogation sessions lasted for a long time, and they were relentless; the police focused in particular on certain phone calls I had received a year before. They showed me dates and times and expected me to remember in detail about the person who had called me, and exactly what we said over the phone. "You're all crazy," I said, losing my temper. "What do you expect me to remember, I don't even know who I talked with yesterday. Cops! Dumb office clerks! Fuck you all!"

"Antonia Villa?"

"Nina Villa."

"Stay calm, Nina Villa."

"I'm very calm."

The policeman who questioned me most often was a bald guy, overweight, but with a likable face and a lazy manner which, I have to admit, in the midst of all that frenzy was pretty agreeable. He would waste time, he'd make jokes, he kept saying Antonia Villa just to make me correct it to Nina Villa. He'd offer me one cup of coffee after another, wander off into tangents, in order to make his points he'd cite either scenes or catch phrases from well known ads or television programs. I was charged with involvement in an armed conspiracy, a very serious crime, but it was a long time before I realized that the only evidence they had was a couple of phone conversations I'd had with Gianna Ostuni, a person I had worked with off and on for a while. It took even longer before I found out that Gianna was somehow involved with the new Red Brigades.

"Your friend is in a world of trouble."

"You guys are as clueless as ever."

"You don't have any faith in your local law enforcement officers?"

"What law?"

"The law of the republic, Antonia Villa."

"Which republic, established by whom, on behalf of whom, and to the irreparable harm of who else?"

The inspector was doing it on purpose, he was trying to provoke me, and I knew it. But that was fine with me: he'd ask questions, and I'd answer rudely, saying as little as possible. It seemed like the right approach.

Had I been in Genoa, in July 2001?

Yes.

With Gianna Ostuni?

Yes.

Did I know Carlo Giuliani?

No.

Had I been involved in the riots?

No.

Why was I there?

To protest against the established order.

What did the established order ever do to hurt you?

We began to discuss the chief world systems, at first quite seriously, but before long making fun of one another. We talked and talked. He never agreed with the points I made, but he never openly disagreed either. Just once he asked me, polemically: "And so you're not a pacifist?"

"I'm in favor of peace."

"Was Carlo Giuliani in favor of peace too?"

"Yes, but you killed him, and you wanted to kill others too."

"So you want all this violence to come to an end."

"Yes."

"How?"

"In the only way possible: with the defeat of the oppressors and the victory of the oppressed."

"Then you're not a pacifist: you want there to be a war and you want it to go on until it ends."

"No, I want peace."

"But you're talking about defeats and victories, Antonia Villa."

"Peace cannot be separated from the defeat of those who buy and sell everything, poisoning the planet, filling arsenals with bombs, and who are willing to blow the whole world sky-high rather than give up their personal privileges, sit down around a table, and give the world a just, free, and peaceful order."

It was after one of these statements that his face lit up and he said:

"Where did you go to high school?"

"At the Liceo Mastronardi."

At this point, he laughed with genuine enjoyment, revealing a mouthful of clean, white teeth.

"That's where I went."

"It's nothing to brag about."

"No. When I went there, there were some awful people teaching classes."

"It was that way when I went there too."

"Do you remember Strimoli?"

"No. By the time I attended, he was gone."

"What about Signora Marruca?"

"I don't know who she is. I graduated ten years ago."

"I'm sad to say that I'm older than you, I got my diploma in 1979. But there's one teacher that we certainly both studied under. I was certain of it when I heard you talk, the words that you use: the oppressed, the oppressors, the disinherited, the humiliated, the abused; this is literature, not politics: who talks like that anymore?"

I looked at him. I immediately felt a sense of annoyance—and anxiety—that was far stronger than the displeasure I felt about the situation I was already in.

"And who do you think this professor is?"

"You already know, I can see it in your face."

"Stasi?"

"Stasi."

"You had Stasi?"

"It shows?"

"A little."

19

They sent me home. I was still under investigation, but Sellitto—now he wanted me to call him by his first name, Augusto—told me that I had no reason to worry. They didn't even have much on Gianna, and if Gianna was clean then I was definitely out of the picture. We would soon be able to go back to our lives, to our work.

"Happy?"

He praised me, said I was a hardworking young woman, for the past six years I had been working as part of a cooperative helping to reintegrate former convicts into society. He said that it was a serious kind of work. Credit to Stasi—I had to admit it—if Sellitto and I, though we were educated and instructed in different periods, had come out with our heads screwed on straight.

I didn't understand right then and there that he was testing the ice. He appeared to be a superficial person, fairly uncultured, cheerfully childish. At times he would pretend to leave the room, then he'd tiptoe back and use a rubber band as a slingshot to fire balls of paper at the lawyer. I saw him firing his little projectiles and then withdrawing, the lawyer would slap at his neck but wouldn't understand, and that would make me laugh. He frequently joked around: with me and with everyone. In contrast, ever since I learned to think, I haven't joked around anymore. It was Stasi who made me incurably serious. Diseased, I would say, diseased with seriousness.

I started to tell him some of the bad things I remembered about our high school professor. I told Sellitto that for me, when he walked into the classroom, it was as if a black cloud had covered the sun, from that moment I lost the carefree nature of my youth. He'd instill a sense in you that life wasn't going to involve any joy. How can you live happily, he used to say, if you know that men, women, and children are forced to spend their lives in inhuman conditions? The only acceptable way of spending our time is to act, act, act to cancel, delete, erase injustice from this world.

"He'd talk," I told Sellitto, "and look at me. Sometimes, when he was calling attendance, I felt the urge to just not answer, or to answer under a different name. Absent or incognito, that's all I desired, to escape him, and not because he wasn't a good teacher, but because he was too good a teacher. Stasi spoke in an amiable tone of voice, he'd show us photographs, reel off statistics from the ancient past, the recent past, and the present, statistics that profoundly disturbed me. He knew everything about everything. I hung from his lips, I hated him and I was grateful to him. He seemed to have a deep wisdom, but his wisdom was like a blast of hot sunlight that ruins the pleasure of a balmy day. When he was in the classroom, I was in a ceaseless state of agitation, wondering: what does he want from me, what does he expect of me? It was a horrible period. I loved him in a way that I've never loved anyone else even now, and yet I feared him, I felt contempt for the way he upset me and overwhelmed me. After I took my diploma I was determined never to see him again.

"Did you know Zara?" Sellitto asked me.

"No, who was he?"

"A guy who, in my day, was a close friend of Stasi's."

"Same type?"

"Worse."

"Meaning?"

"They talked in a way that when I was a kid, at the time, I thought: these people are determined and important, at the very minimum they are part of the strategic leadership of the Red Brigades."

We both started to laugh.

Many stories emerged from both our experiences at that high school—certain old war horses that Stasi seemed obsessed with: Petrarch's *Secretum*, Boccaccio's "Novella of the Fat Woodcutter," the identities of those seated at Don Rodrigo's dining room table when Fra Cristoforo arrives in Manzoni's *The Betrothed*—stories that were funny but also instructive, manners of speech, his own axioms. Sellitto said that the other guy, Zara, hadn't been the source of anything positive for him. Once, he'd come dangerously close to a fistfight with Zara—he was sixteen, and his high school professor was thirty. Fortunately it turned out that the asshole was a childhood friend of one of Sellitto's uncles, so it was all taken care of, he didn't flunk him for the year. Then, thank God, Zara left, he really never should have become a teacher at all. Stasi, on the other hand, was very good at his job, he was a completely different kind of person, he had a first-rate mind, he could gather information and analyze it, he had a profound ethical foundation.

"Are you sure of that?"

"Yes."

"I don't know."

I told him that talking about Stasi depressed me, and it was the truth. He was there in my words, my thoughts, even now I acted in the hope that he would approve what I did.

"Does he know that you've become a cop?"

"No."

"If he ever found out, he'd refuse to shake your hand."

"I doubt that."

I went to live with my parents. I was still very upset, I had no desire to go back to my apartment. Friends and relatives had called, there had been an outpouring of solidarity, no one had believed even for a moment that I might really be involved, even remotely, in acts of violence. My mother told that even my old literature professor had called.

"Stasi?"

I lost my temper, I really reacted badly. I screamed at her, at my brother and my father, that if Stasi called back they should tell him I wasn't interested in talking to anyone. But I was still living with my parents when he called again. While my brother talked to him, I sat in a corner and hated myself for the storm of emotion that swelled in my chest, in my veins.

Then one day I heard someone call my name in the street. It was Sellitto. He looked as if he found something very amusing. He said that if he hadn't chanced to run into me, he would certainly have called me. He had had an idea.

"What's your idea?" I asked.

"Let's give Stasi a mission to perform."

"A mission?"

He asked me to have lunch with him. It was as if he had regressed to the years of high school, and he infected me, I regressed to those years with him. He said that he had undertaken a little investigation of his own, that this guy, Zara, Luciano Zara, was now a well regarded pianist, his executions of the music of Liszt were highly considered among the cognoscenti. He was going to give a recital at the Hotel Hassler on March 26 for certain friends of his, a group of highfalutin intellectuals, a couple of weeks from today.

"Well, what of it?"

He laughed, he looked at me with a particularly cunning expression: "What do you think of when you hear the word 'execution'?"

20

His idea was to put Stasi in the condition of a terrorist. He wanted to place him, gradually, step by step, face to face with his intended victim, and see if Stasi was enough of a coward—that's right, enough of a coward—to pull the trigger.

"And who's going to be the victim?"

"The other jerk, Comrade Zara. We'll set them up, one against the other, face-to-face."

I sat there listening to him, perplexed. Did he really mean it? I couldn't tell. He was one of those people who know how to conceal their real intentions. You sense that those intentions are there, one step back, lying in ambush behind their very words, their gestures, their courteous manners. However, I have to admit, he convinced me of one thing: as we talked about Stasi's teachings, he experienced the same devoted suffering that I did, the same enamored resentment. Before he had spoken of Stasi affectionately, now he called him a dickhead. We talked about it for a long time. The marks that that man had left upon both of us ran deep. We both attributed to him a naïve harshness, present in every word he said. We both considered ourselves contented victims of the inimitable way he had of creating in our heads an entire world inspired by his world. Both of us—we discovered—had long and secretly suspected that Stasi was a gullible impostor, that his way of depicting himself was seductive precisely because it was invented out of whole cloth, for our edification and consumption, and for his own.

"Either Stasi is an honest and serious person, in which case he is a danger to himself and to those around him, or else he is fooling himself, and if that's the case, then what are you and I? The creations of a con artist, a fraud?" Sellitto said to me, surprising me with the grimace of pain that I sensed in his mocking words.

"And so?"

He wanted me to meet the professor, and then ask him to do something for me with a conspiratorial air: for example, go get a book in an apartment, and transmit a password to someone else.

"Why?"

"To see if he agrees to do it or refuses."

"And if he agrees?"

"If he does it, then we'll keep the game going."

"How far?"

"To the point that we provide him with a pistol, loaded with blanks, and we send him over to the Hotel Hassler."

"And then?"

"We'll see, it'll be up to him. Either he'll sit down harmlessly in a corner and listen to his former comrade performing Liszt, or else he'll shoot him."

"And if he shoots him?"

Sellitto gave me an ironic glance:

"The question isn't whether or not he shoots. The question is whether or not he surprises us."

We avoided discussing or wondering what would have surprised him and what would have surprised me, and whether we would both have been surprised by the same thing. He looked at me with boyish eyes, as if to say: come on, let's do it, he tormented us for years, the time has come for us to torment him for a while. I was tempted. To finally excavate Stasi from decades of words. Make him experience the burden, the responsibility, the delirium of doing. I said: "Okay, where do we send him?"

"The uncle I mentioned, the one who used to know Zara, now he teaches in America, his name is Carlo Corace. He has an apartment in Via Pavia, I have the key. Let's send him there."

"To get what?"

"That I couldn't say, I don't know anything about books. You have to find a novel and a quote from it."

I thought for a moment, then I said:

"*The Death of Virgil.*"

"I don't know it, but that's fine. What about the quote?"

"Let me think."

We ate, we drank, I really enjoyed myself.

Sellitto viewed this experiment as amusing, to me before long it seemed like a crucial, decisive turning point. Afterward, I would vanish, I hoped never to have further dealings with him. But for the moment, I was fully involved, planning, laughing, insisting. I sensed that I urgently needed to know. I wanted to discover whether Stasi would really go to pick up the book for me, if he would climb from station to station to the point of ultimately pulling the trigger. And I clearly perceived, to my surprise, that if he were to do it, I would lose faith, something inside would be definitively broken, with untold and perhaps untellable consequences.

The three years of school with him were hard. He often quoted from the Gospels, even though he said he was not a believer, and he did it as if it was only a tool to blunt slogans that he found irritating or to debunk trite formulations. He chose his words not as a way of conveying rules or information to us, but to mark us deeply. He used to say: I can only plant the seed, then everything depends on the soil in which it lies. There is barren soil and fertile soil. And you can never be sure of what will happen even with the fertile soil. One patch of soil yields thirty, another might yield sixty, and another still might yield a hundred. He wanted us all to yield one hundred. The burden of that expectation weighed more heavily on me than on the others. I detested him not for what he taught us, but for the way I suffered at the idea that I might not be up to his highest expectations, the expectations that I thought he left unstated, in the spaces between the words, specifically because he wanted me—me and no one else—to sense their scope and achieve them. I defended myself from him by relegating him to the world of his words, his phrases, that was his territory, I would say, that was where he was powerful but he could never go beyond that boundary, a place of admiration but nothing concrete. No, Stasi wouldn't shoot, he was incapable of it. Rather, he was the authoritative figure that you needed to protect in battle, a leader you had to save so that afterwards he could pin a medal to your chest, with just and moving words, a medal that would fill you with pride.

I said goodbye to Sellitto, kissing him on both cheeks. Nearly everything had been decided, he was beside himself with excitement.

"Let's make sure of the book; we don't want to send him to Via Pavia and not have him find this *Death of Virgil*."

I reassured him, I'd get the book myself. I really wanted it to be that title, Stasi had spoken of it twelve years ago in a respectful, inspired tone. He had loaned me the book himself and I had never returned it to him, I still had it. I wondered if he remembered that. He had given it to me with such a solemn air that I thought: it must be a wonderful book.

"And was it a wonderful book?"

"I was fifteen years old, it bored me."

"Then let's find a more cheerful book."

"No, I don't think so."

I turned to go. Then I stopped for a moment and looked back at him. He was short, hatless, with big ears, an apparently ridiculous little man. But, I noticed, he had a cautious watchful air, the taut gait of a dangerous individual. The only thing we had in common was Stasi. Now, we were about to place our old high school teacher in a humiliating situation and we found this at the same time amusing and worrisome. A prank always carries with it high margins of risk both for the victim and for the pranksters. Sellitto and I knew that we were not only mocking Stasi's whole life, but that we were putting in play the basic meaning of our own lives. I clearly sensed that he hoped the professor really would use the gun, so that he could feel he was superior to his teacher, to prove to Stasi how necessary his own work really was, to be able to say to him with respectful sarcasm: I owe everything to you, your lessons taught me the urgent necessity of restraint and repression. In contrast, I hoped with every ounce of my being that the professor would not shoot, because I had assumed for years the responsibility of doing it in his place, in compliance with the necessity that he had shown me, but to which he would never have been capable of bending himself.

There were times, when it was dark in the apartment and I was so forgetful that I forgot to turn on the lights, when I would see my two students bending over the sheets of paper that they used to sketch out their plan against me.

There was no humor, they never laughed. They seemed like a pair of old people, their faces marked like mine by their good deeds and their bad ones, and I wasn't particularly happy about still being in their thoughts, they struck me as thoughts under dark veils.

I wanted to erase them. They had put me in a strange situation unsuited to these times, to my real way of thinking. I could no longer apply a serious thread of narrative to my own life. Phrases that had once seemed solid snapped in two before I could utter them.

For a long time, I worked with no real sense of interest, aiming only to reach the end and put together an over-all map of the possibilities of the story. A text really only defines itself during the second draft, when I read it again from beginning to end, and I understand where I really wanted to take it, and I toss out hypotheses, I rewrite, I polish and shape, I find more effective words.

Was it really necessary to return to Nina in such extensive detail?

Was it really necessary to end the book with a short chapter devoted to Stasi and his reaction to Sellitto and Nina Villa's prank?

Nina, isn't that a kind of ordinary name? Didn't Antonia sound better, Antonia Villa?

I made a list of the things that I wanted to change, I multi-plied the number of white spaces, creating islands of writing to examine, perhaps to eliminate.

Once, with a vague sense of worry, I thought of Mina; she hadn't phoned again. To some extent I was pleased, but I was also somehow a little sorry. On certain sluggish days I felt that that story, if I worked on it, could become clearer, even more meaningful, than the story of Stasi. Or perhaps I should say: Stasi was doing fine, he was ready; in fact, if needed, he could even exit the story of Nina and enter the story of Mina.

Only then, with the two names next to one another, did I

notice that they rhymed. Wasn't it curious that they should be so similar?

Hmmm, I would change Nina's name to Antonia.

One afternoon, at a poetry reading, I met Antonella Anedda. She was waiting for her turn to read. She was as elegant as a question mark, cheerful, and a bit lost. She let me read the verses she planned to read over the microphone, and I liked them. She had a book ready, she said, *From the Terrace of the Body;* Mondadori was going to publish it soon. I tried to tell her the main points of the story I was writing, but I regretted it immediately, stories die if you try to tell them before you are done writing them. I said: "When it's ready I'll let you read it." I praised the title of her book, I had admired her verse for decades. Sometimes she would read them to me over the phone, and I would imagine the words, recently dropped onto the page, like live fish caught in a net.

She sent me a part of the *Terrace of the Body* by e-mail, and I read things filled with distant resonances and echoes. I called her and I read to her poems that she had written that had moved me. I had immediately grown to love certain of her poems for no clear reason:

Squint your eyes, and know from where terror comes.
From the nail in yesterday's tree trunk
From that mushroom at night exploded
From an enormous chestnut tree.

Somehow, we wound up talking about when we were children, about each of our childhoods. We joked and laughed. She is someone who knows how to laugh.

"When I was small, I wanted to work in a filling station. I would spend the whole day reading, enclosed in the little glass cage, while outside the wind howled and the rain poured down," I said.

"I wanted to open a linen shop," she told me.

She liked the smell of clean linen, she liked the feel of it. "Every time I walk past a hotel," she told me, "I feel like checking into a room, getting into bed, and sleeping between fresh sheets for the rest of the day."

The image pleased me. Falling into the fresh scent of the sheets, falling asleep in cleanliness. I was trying to write about it with the words that she had used—I felt that Anedda's idea of sleeping in the daytime, in pure cleanliness, could help me to establish a feeling of Stasi's that was still muddled—when the intercom buzzed from the street.

It was getting dark, the apartment was in shadow. The only light was from the computer, I was touch typing. Outside it was raining. I shouted to my wife: "Are you going to get it?"

"You go see who it is—I'm taking a shower."

I stood up from my desk with a groan, my neck and my back both ached. There was just a narrow shaft of light at the bottom of the bathroom door. The water dripping onto the shower floor blended with the sound of raindrops against the windows. I moved through the dark, and out of laziness didn't bother to turn on the lights. I pressed the button on the intercom.

"Yes?"

"Professor?"

"Yes."

"I have a package for you: can you come down for a moment? I couldn't find any place to park."

"Just leave it on the mailbox."

"Sorry, I need a signature."

I was distracted, I was cold, and I still couldn't match myself with myself, Anedda with Anedda, or Stasi with Stasi.

"Okay, I'm coming down."

I walked down the steps to the main street entrance. I walked slowly downstairs, I wanted to give the words time to fade. I pushed the button and clicked open the door. I found myself face to face with two men wearing rain jackets and hoods, the rain was drumming down on them. I recognized one of them. He was the man who resembled the man with whom I'd had that run-in on the bus some time before. He said, in an emotional voice, but without menace:

"My father is dead."

Clearly, there was no delivery for me, only that piece of news.

"When?"

"This morning."

"I'm sorry."

The other man said in a calm tone of voice:

"We want you to see him."

"Why?"

He pointed to the man at his side, who was staring at me, with questioning eyes, as if he were trying to understand whether I was really myself: "It would make my brother-in-law happy."

"When?"

"Now."

The son of the man I had attacked spoke again, but this time choked by a sentiment that I could not immediately identify: agitation, anger:

"You behaved badly, with my father. You need to see him now, his face is the face of innocence."

"Perhaps I only exaggerated," I said, then I added: "But I'm happy to come. I'll tell my wife and get my raincoat."

The pair exchanged a glance, the quiet man said: "Go ahead, we'll wait here for you."

Acknowledgement

The books that I write belong to me from the first word to the last, and therefore I never thank others at the end. Now, however, I would like to make an exception. I am very grateful to Annalisa Agrati who held together materials from different periods and intentions—files, notebooks, notes, e-mails, text messages, jottings done with a ball point pen on the palm of the hand—with an ironic sense of discretion, with courteous firmness, without ever saying—except with a cheerful sense of humor: what does this have to do with that? why is the face broad here and slender here? why is the narrator first "I" and then "he" and then, a little further along, "I" again? It is pleasant, in times like these, to work with a person who is capable of helping you without saying that you wrote a piece of nonsense but that instead, she has a doubt and would like to share it with you. This, however, does not absolve me from all responsibility. It goes without saying that I am guilty of all nonsense and foolishness, and that if there are some good lines in this book, I myself suspect that credit should be attributed to Signora Agrati.

ABOUT THE AUTHOR

Domenico Starnone was born in Naples in 1943 and now lives in Rome. He is the author of eight novels and numerous books of non-fiction. In 2001, he was the recipient of Italy's most prestigious literary prize, the Strega.